Elise Lathrop, Ossip Schubin

Asbeïn, from the Life of a Virtuoso

Elise Lathrop, Ossip Schubin

Asbeïn, from the Life of a Virtuoso

ISBN/EAN: 9783337056230

Printed in Europe, USA, Canada, Australia, Japan

Cover: Foto ©Raphael Reischuk / pixelio.de

More available books at **www.hansebooks.com**

ASBEÏN

FROM THE LIFE OF A VIRTUOSO

BY

OSSIP SCHUBIN

TRANSLATED BY ÉLISE L. LATHROP

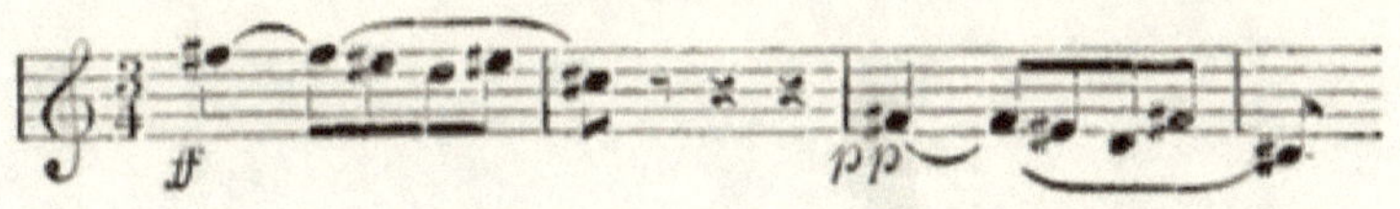

NEW YORK
WORTHINGTON CO., 747 BROADWAY
1890

Press of J. J. Little & Co.,
Astor Place, New York.

ASBEÏN.*

FIRST BOOK.

" BUT—do you really not recognize me ?"
With these words, and with friendly, outstretched hands, a young lady hastened
toward a man who, with gloomily contracted brow, wrapped in thought, went on
his way without noticing either her or his
surroundings. He was foolish, for his surroundings were picturesque—Rome, near
the Fontana di Trevi, on a bright March

---

* When the Devil, banished from heaven, resolved on
the temptation of mankind, he loved to make use of
music which had been made known to him as a heavenly
privilege when he still was a member of the eternal hosts.
But the Almighty deprived him of his memory, so he could
remember but a single strain, and this mysterious, bewitching strain is still called in Arabia " The Devil's
Strain—Asbeïn."—*Arabian Legends.*

afternoon. And the young lady—she was charming.

Although she had called to him in French, something about her—one could scarcely have told what—betrayed the Russian; everything, the pampered woman from the highest circles of society.

The young man whose attention she had sought to attract in such a violent and unconventional manner was just as evidently a Russian, but of quite a different condition. One could hardly decide to what fixed sphere of society he belonged, but one perceived immediately that his manners had never been improved, polished, softened by society discipline, that he was no man of the world. He was, evidently, a man who was apart from the rank and file, a man who stood far out from the conventional frame, a man whom no one could pass without twice looking after him. His form was large and somewhat heavy; his face, framed by dark, half-curled hair, in spite of the blunt profile, reminded one of

Napoleon Bonaparte, but Bonaparte in the
first romantic period of his life, before he
had become fat and accustomed to pose for
the classic head of Cæsar.

She was the Princess Natalie Alexandrovna Assanow; he the fêted violin virtuoso
and well-known composer, Boris Lensky.

She had run herself quite out of breath
to catch up with him; twice she had called
to him before he heard her; then he looked
around and lifted his hat.

"Boris Nikolaivitch, do you not really
recognize me?" said she, now in Russian,
laughing and breathless.

"You here, Princess! Since when?
Why have you given me no sign of your
existence?" and he took both the slender
girlish hands, still outstretched to him, in
his.

"We only arrived here yesterday from
Naples."

"Ah! and I go there to-day." His long-
drawn words betrayed very significantly a
certain vexation.

"Yes, to give three concerts there. I know; it was in the newspapers," she nodded earnestly, and sighed.

"Hm!" he began; "then—" he hesitated.

"Then you do not understand why I did not wait for the concerts?" said she, gayly; "it was impossible."

"Impossible?" said he with a short, defiant motion of the head, the motion of a too-tightly checked race-horse who impatiently jerks at the bridle. "How so impossible? What word is that from the mouth of a young lady who has nothing else in the world to do but amuse herself?"

"As if I were independent!" she sighed, with comic despair. "First, mamma could not leave Naples—hm—for family reasons. My sister is married there, you know. Then—then——"

"Do not trouble yourself with polite excuses," he interrupted her. "I see that you are no longer interested in my music;" and, half-jesting, half-vexed, shrugging his shoulders, he added, "What of it? One must put up with one's destiny!"

"I am no longer interested in your music!" said she, angrily; "and you venture to say that to me, even after I have run after you—yes, really run after you, which is not proper—only to——"

She stopped, her face wore a vexed, indignant expression. "Why did you do it?" said he, roughly; "it is not becoming."

Instead of losing her self-possession, she laughed heartily. "But, Boris Nikolaivitch," said she, "you speak as if you were a true man of the world. However, as you please, I thank you for the lecture. Adieu!"

And nodding her head quite arrogantly, she was about to turn on her heel, when her look met his. She saw that she had vexed him, remained standing, blushed, and lowered her eyes.

The waters of the Acqua Nigo foamed and sparkled gayly between the edges of the stone basin which Nicolo Salvi had made for them ; the noonday church-bells mingled their deep, solemn voices with the caressing rippling of the waves ; the sun shone full from the deep-blue, ice-cold heaven, a glaring, unpleasant March sun, which was light without warming, like the condescending smile of a great man, and Natalie's maid who, grumbling and bored, stood a step behind her young mistress, opened a round, green fan to shield her eyes, and at the same time stamped her feet from the cold. Around, the Roman life went on in its usual lazy way. Before a small, loaded cart stood a mule with a number of red and blue tassels about its ears and on its forehead hung a brass image of the Virgin. In the door of a vegetable shop, from which came a strong smell of herbs, crouched a black-eyed, white Spitz dog, that twitched its right ear uneasily. A fat, smooth-headed Capuchin passed by, then came two shabbily dressed young people. The Capuchin stopped to scratch the mule's head, the young people nudged each other, and said in an undertone, while they pointed to the virtuoso : " *E Borisso Lensky.*"

" There you have it," said the princess, shaking off her vexation with a charming, pleasant smile, and her head bent one side. "Great man that you are, and still you take it amiss in me." She said nothing more, only raised her great blue eyes and gave him a look, a never-to-be-forgotten look, behind whose roguishness a riddle was concealed.

" I take nothing amiss in you," said he, earnestly.

" Really nothing? Now, then, I can tell you how much, oh! how much, I have longed to hear you play again, that I, *coûte qu'il coûte*, seized the opportunity to ask you to stop in Rome on your return from Naples only to—" She hesitated, as if she were suddenly afraid of being indiscreet.

" Only to play something for the Princess Natalie Alexandrovna Assanow," he completed her sentence, laughing. " Good. I will come, Natalie Alexandrovna ; in two weeks I am there. But if you are then in Florence or Nice——"

She was about to make a very positive assertion, when a slender, fashionably dressed man, with a very high hat and faultless gloves, passed by them, greeted the princess respectfully, and, with a slight squint, measured Lensky from head to foot. Lensky recognized in him an officer of the guard, Count Konstantin Paulovitch Pachotin, and remembered last winter, during the season in St. Petersburg, he paid court to Natalie. The scrutinizing look of the young man vexed him beyond bounds ; everything looked red before him. "Ah! he here?" he asked the young princess with mocking emphasis. "May one congratulate you?"

She frowned and turned away her head. "No!" murmured she. Then raising her wonderful eyes to him again : " So, farewell for two weeks!"

" Perhaps."

" Say positively, I beg you, and throw the traditional soldo in the fountain."

"With the best of intentions, I cannot do that; I have none with me," he laughed, now involuntarily.

She was charming. She wore a brown velvet bonnet that was fastened under the chin with broad ribbons. She had pushed back her veil, and the transparent brown gauze shining in the sun formed a golden background for her pretty, pale face. It was cold, although the beginning of March, and therefore her tall figure was wrapped to the feet in a sable-trimmed velvet cloak, beneath which a scarcely visible silk dress rustled very melodramatically. A delicate perfume of amber and fresh violets exhaled from her.

"You have no soldo?" said she; "then I will lend you one." She earnestly sought in her portemonnaie, whereupon she handed him the coin. He threw it in the basin of the noisy, rippling Fontana di Trevi. The water sparkled golden for a moment, when the coin sank, and tried to form circles, but the spouting gayety of the cascade obliterated them.

"You will come!" said Natalie, laughing gayly.

"Yes, I will come," said he, not gayly as she, but gloomily, even grumbling. "But if you are not there," he added, "or——."

She had already turned to go, and without replying anything to his last words, she called to him over her shoulder:

"*Via Giulia Palazzo Morsini!*"

He looked after her for a long time. The fashionable dress at that time was very ugly. This little scene took place in the fifties, when the Empress Eugenie had again brought into favor the hoop-skirt which had disappeared quite a half-century before. But still Natalie Alexandrovna was charming. How peculiar her walk was, so light and still a little dragging, dreamily gliding, withal not weary, but with a peculiar certain characteristic rhythm. He thoughtfully hummed a melody to it.

Yes, he would come back. Whether he would have come back if the glance of the

officer of the guard had not angered him?
He must see, must teach this dandy!

.   .   .   .   .   .

" You speak just as if you were a true man
of the world," the princess had replied to
his—as he angrily told himself—highly unsuitable and tasteless advice. Now it might
perhaps be small ; yes, certainly it was small,
but sometimes, sometimes he would secretly have preferred to be a true man of the
world instead of being—a celebrity.

"She ran after me ! " he said to himself
again. "Why did she run after me? It was
charming in her—she would not have done
it for any one else! Bah! She is still only
like all the others!" And the great artist,
whose life resembled a continual triumphal
procession, of whom already a finger-thick
biography with glaringly false dates had appeared, and concerning whom the papers
every day reported something remarkable,
suddenly felt a kind of envy of Count Konstantin Paulovitch Pachotin, a St. Petersburg dandy, whose name had never been in

the papers, and **whom** he despised for his narrow-mindedness.

He was a great genius, but, like **many** other great geniuses, he was of quite obscure parentage. Some asserted **he came from** that horrible citadel of the poor in Moscow **where misery** intrenches itself against prog-**ress, in** filth, stupidity, and **vice**; others said he had been found, a scarcely week-old child, wrapped in rags, before **the door of** the Conservatory in St. Petersburg. There were really all kinds of accounts in the pa-pers. **This one said that** he was the son of a princess of the blood and a **gypsy**; that **one, that** he descended from an old princely family of the Czechs, and many other such romantic inventions. He shrugged **his** shoulders scornfully at all such improvisa-tions, without refuting them by accurate personal accounts. How did the cold, hun-gry, maltreated sadness of his **first youth concern** the world? **Now** he was **Boris** Lensky, one of the first musicians of his time. Everything else could be indifferent to the man. It was indifferent to them; it was quite indifferent to them all, only not to him. The wounds which the tormenting martyrdom of his childhood had torn in his heart had never quite healed; therefore he showed a sensitiveness and irritability which even the most sympathetic person could scarcely comprehend.

But now he fared very well in the world. No one was so pampered, so caressed as he.

His playing exercised such a penetrating, sense-ensnaring charm that his listeners, transported in a kind of musical intoxication, lost their capability of judging, and even the most well-bred women crowded around him with allegiance so exaggerated that it tore down the boundary of every customary demeanor.

Another would have enjoyed this allegiance without thinking further of it; but for Lensky, on the contrary, it had a repellent effect. Child of the people to the finger-tips, totally unused to the customs of

fashionable circles, his feeling of propriety
was as wounded by what he plainly called
insolent shamelessness as that of a peasant
who for the first time sees a woman with
bare shoulders.

Besides his sense of propriety, there was
another that was wounded by the lack of
reserve which great ladies showed him, and
that was his pride. Not only gifted with
musical genius, but with a very clear head,
he soon perceived that if the ladies of the
great world permitted themselves freer
manners with him than did women of a
more modest sphere of life, they still took
liberties with him of which they would have
been ashamed in association with companions of their own rank. "*Mon dieu, avec un
virtuose, cela ne tire pas à conséquence,*" he
once heard an elegant little St. Petersburg
woman say. He never forgot the words, and
in consequence received all the feminine allegiance of good society with hostile distrust.

He usually excused the tactless exuber-
ance of a poorly cared for, badly brought

up woman of the Conservatory. In society
of this kind, of saddened womanly existence, incessantly touched with pity, he
showed kindness to the sad enthusiasts
wherever he could, and laughed at their
tasteless animation. But for the great ladies, who should have known better, who
thought that they alone held the monopoly of good form, and who still pursued a
man like wild beasts—for these he had no
consideration. His roughness in intercourse with them had become almost as
proverbial as the success which he attained
with them.

Still, in his home he quite unconsciously
accustomed himself to an aristocratic atmosphere, and, with the refined sense of a true
artist nature, susceptible to all beauty and
distinction, in association with great ladies
he felt a mixture of irritation and pleasure,
while pleasure gradually won the upper
hand; and in foreign countries, where he
was received only exceptionally and with
official solemnity, and really had intimate

access to salons of the second rank only, he renounced intercourse with that refined world which he abused, like so many others, without being able to escape its perfidious charm, and felt, every time that he met one of his despised pretty St. Petersburg or Moscow enthusiasts, an unmistakable joy.

Two weeks after his meeting with Natalie at the Fontana di Trevi, Lensky appeared for the first time in the Palazzo Morsini. From a very large staircase, whose beauties he must admire by the light of the wax matches which he had brought in his pocket, he stumbled into a large vestibule, from which the servant conducted him through a heavy portière, painted with coats of arms as high as a man, into an immense drawing-room with soiled and faded yellow damask hangings and furniture.

"Monsieur Lensky!" announced the servant.

The virtuoso was accustomed to a universal exclamation following the announcement of his name, and the looks of the whole assembly should be directed to him.

Nothing of the sort this time. Natalie sat near an old French lady, Marquise de C., whose knitting she kindly helped to arrange, and as the young Russian introduced the virtuoso to her, she raised her lorgnette and said : " Monsieur Lensky—ah ! *vraiment, that is very interesting !* " whereupon, without further troubling herself about him, she continued to speak to Natalie of all kinds of social affairs, the marriage of Marie X., the debts of Alexander T., the trousseau of Aurelie Z., and the boldness of that parvenu A.

For the present he could not approach the hostess. She warded him off with a nod from the distance, for she was engaged in a very exciting occupation. Although the universal interest for spiritualistic table-tapping and moving was already quite over, the repetition of this experiment, which strangely enough often succeeded in the

Palazzo Morsini, was one of the favorite pastimes of Natalie's mother, the Princess Irina Dimitrievna Assanow. She now sat at a table in the middle of the drawing-room between many others, most of them old Russians, men and women ; opposite her a thin, very young man with long, straight, blond hair, a well-known magnetizer.

It seemed to Lensky as if he had never seen anything more laughable than these half-dozen almost exclusively gray-haired people who sat with solemn bearing and attentive faces around a table whose edge they could just surround with hands stretched out as far as possible.

Those present who did not directly participate in the attempt to bewitch the table, stood around observing the interesting round surface.

But the table continued in a state of desperately exciting passivity.

Lensky, usually specially invited to soirées, of which he formed the centre of attraction, felt humiliated by the four-legged wooden rival, who, to-day, took all the attention away from him.

At last the old French woman turned to the observation of the table, which permitted the young girl to devote herself a little to Lensky, rapidly becoming more gloomy; then the door opened and the butler announced Count Pachotin. The virtuoso felt not at all pleasantly toward the young dandy when he asked him unusually kindly and sympathetically whether he was contented with the result of his last concert tour.

After Pachotin had fulfilled the condescension, which as a finely cultivated nobleman he thought he owed to an artistic star he turned to Natalie and from then ignored Lensky as completely as the Marquise de C. had done. Lensky meanwhile morosely pulled long horse-hairs from the holes in the thread-bare arms of the damask chair. He was very helpless in spite of his already great renown. His actions in society were solely confined to playing and permitting the ladies to rave over him. He did not understand how to take an inconspicuous part in the conversation, and to cross the room for any other purpose than to take up his violin made him quite giddy.

The table meanwhile still refused to move. The excitement became general.

"*Voyons*, M. Lensky," called the Marquise de C., suddenly turning to the young artist, lorgnette at her eyes; "if you should give us a little music perhaps it would act upon the legs of this stiff-necked table."

A man quick at repartee would have answered the silly remark with a gay jest. But Lensky grew deathly pale, sprang up; in that moment the resisting sacrifice of magnetism began to totter and tremble.

Even Pachotin left his place near Natalie in order to watch closely the interesting spectacle. The magnetizers rose and, with earnest, triumphant faces, accompanied the table, which now seemed to have entered into the spirit of the affair and took the most remarkable steps with its wooden legs.

"I CANNOT LET YOU GO AWAY ANGRY," SAID SHE.

p. 23.

"*Vous partez déjà?*" asked Natalie, coming up to the virtuoso.

"I am no longer needed," said Lensky, with a glance at the table, and bowed without touching the outstretched hand of the young girl.

Without, in the vestibule just as he was about to put his arms in the overcoat which the servant held out to him, he saw the princess, who had hastened after him.

"I cannot let you go away angry," said she. "Come to-morrow to lunch. We never receive in the morning, but you will be welcome."

This time he took her hand in his, and looked in her eyes with a peculiar mixture of anger and tenderness.

"You know I do everything that you wish," murmured he; "but——"

"Well?" She smiled pleasantly and encouragingly. He turned away his head and went.

"Perhaps in reality she is only like the others, but still she is bewitching!" he murmured, as he stumbled down the old marble steps of the palace in the darkness.

.   .   .   .   .   .

Yes, she was bewitching. Many still remember how charming she was at that time. She was from Moscow, and a true Moscow woman; that is to say, deeper, more polished, more intellectual, than the average St. Petersburg woman, whom a pert Frenchman has described as "*Parisiennes à la sauce tartare.*" Lensky had met her the former year at her relatives' in Petersburg, where they had sent her for the ball season, perhaps with the idea that she would make a good match.

Her domestic circumstances were quite disturbed. Her mother, a former beauty, and who in her youth had been much admired at the court of Alexander I., could not adapt herself to her poverty—that is to say, she absolutely could not exist on the very moderate remains of a splendid property which her husband had squandered. She never complained; she only never kept within her means. She was always planning new reforms, but her most saving plans always proved costly when carried out.

When she summoned Natalie home from St. Petersburg the former May she had just formed a quite special resolution: she would travel to a foreign country, in order, as she expressed it, to be unconstrainedly shabby and economical. Her unconstrained shabbiness in Rome consisted in living in a very picturesque *palazzo* with two maids brought with her from Russia, a male factotum, and a number of Italian assistants; by day, clad in a faded sky-blue *peignoir*, stretched on a lounge, alternately reading French novels and playing patience; in the evening, receiving an amusing assembly of *gens du monde* and celebrities, among whom the already mentioned magnetizer enjoyed her especial sympathy, at dinner or tea. Her economy culminated in locking up the most trifling articles with great punctilious- ness and never being able to find the keys;

for which reason the locksmith must be frequently summoned.

The Russian maids naturally never moved their hands, the Italian assistants wiped the dust from one piece of furniture to another, and so the household would really have made quite an impression of having come down in the world if the butler, whom they had brought with them had not saved it by his aristocratic prestige. A Frenchman and valet of the deceased prince, Monsieur Baptiste was not only outwardly decorative, but of a useful nature. His principal occupation consisted in sitting in the vestibule, with finely-shaved upper lip and imposing side-whiskers, intrenched behind a newspaper, and overpowering the creditors if they ventured to present their unpaid bills.

. . . . . .

Lensky had resolved to leave Rome the next day, and to ignore the invitation of the princess. Returned to the hotel, he immediately set about packing; that is to say, he in all haste wrapped and squeezed his effects together in any manner and threw them in his trunk as one throws potatoes in a sack. Then he ordered his bill from the waiter and a carriage for the next morning. When the waiter at the appointed hour presented the bill and announced the carriage he showed him out. From ten o'clock on he drew out his chronometer every quarter of an hour; at twelve he appeared in the Palazzo Morsini.

"You are punctual," said the princess, stretching out her hand to him; "that is nice of you. I was terribly afraid that you would not come. We are quite among ourselves; only mamma and we two. Does that suit you?"

Again she bent her head to one side and looked at him with that peculiar glance, behind whose roguishness a riddle was concealed. What was it? Something sweet, perhaps something tender, earnest—or only a gay triumph or planned conquest?

Meanwhile it cost him the greatest self-restraint not to fall at her feet immediately, so charming and beautiful was she. Everything about her was beautiful: her tall but beautifully rounded figure; her pale oval face, framed in dark hair; her remarkable eyes, usually dreamily half closed, and then suddenly looking at one so large and full; her long small hands and her little feet. No Andalusian had a smaller, slenderer, more finely-arched foot than Natalie. He had scarcely time to reply to her amiability, when the butler announced that luncheon was served, and they went into the dining-room.

It was a peculiar luncheon. The old princess presided in a wrapper. The luke-warm dishes—brought every day from a restaurant in a tin box, which Lensky had met on the steps—were served by Monsieur Baptiste on the largely shattered remnants of a Florentine faïence service with noticeable correctness. A broad golden sunbeam lay on the table between Lensky and Nata-

lie and gave the most extravagantly unsuitable colors to the flowers which shed their
fragrance from a low Japanese porcelain
bowl in the middle of the table, and over
these flowers, sparkling like diamonds, he
looked at her.

She ate little and talked a great deal,
told all kinds of droll stories ; one witty an-
ecdote followed the other. He could not
weary of listening to her. Yes, even if what
she said had not interested him, he would
not tire of hearing her. The sweet, somewhat veiled tone of her voice seemed like a
caress to his sensitive ear.

.   .   .   .

" I would like to ask you something, Boris
Nikolaivitch," said the old princess later,
while they were taking coffee, in the drawing-room.

" I am at your disposition entirely, Princess," Lensky hastened to assure her.

" It is about my violins," she began, in a
drawling, whining voice, which was her
manner, and meant nothing.

" But, mamma," Natalie hastily interrupted her, " this is not the moment——"

" Pray, permit me," said Lensky ; and turning to the princess, " so it is about your violins?"

" Yes.   My husband—you know what an excellent player he was," continued the old lady, " has left three violins.   People have always told me they were worth a small fortune, but I did not wish to part with them at any price.   I ask you—a souvenir. But finally—times are hard, and one must not be too hard on the peasants, and, besides, as none of my children play the violin, however musical they are—well, I would be very glad if you would try the instruments and incidentally value them. You could perhaps advise me—yes—— What is the matter, Natascha?"

For Natalie had blushed to the roots of her hair.   Tears stood in her eyes.

Boris guessed that she feared he would look upon the explanation of her mother as a bid.

" I remember the violins very well," he hastened to assure her ; " especially one of them excited my envy. It would please me very much to try them again."

The servant brought the violins and at the same time a pile of hastily snatched-up violin music, smelling of dust, dampness, and camphor. The wonderfully beautiful instruments were in a pitiable condition— half of the strings were gone, those that remained were brittle and dry. But still there was a small stock of them. After Boris, with the loving patience and surgical skill with which only a true violinist handles an Amati, had put it in a suitable condition and then tuned it, he drew the bow softly across it. A strangely sweet, tender, sad sound vibrated through the great empty room. It seemed as if the violin awoke with a sigh from an enchanted sleep. A pleasant shudder passed over Natalie.

Lensky bent his cheek to the splendid instrument like a lover. " Shall we try something ?" said he, and took from the pile of notes a nocturne of Chopin, transposed for the violin, opened the piano, the only good and costly piece of furniture in the room, and laid the notes on the music-rack. "Now, Natalie Alexandrovna, may I beg you?"

Quite frightened by his artistic greatness—yes, trembling from charming embarrassment—she sat down at the piano.

His violin began to sing; how full and soft, so delightfully languishing, and also somewhat veiled, as is usually the case with an instrument unused for years.

"How beautiful!" murmured Natalie, with eyes sparkling with animation.

"Yes, it is a splendid instrument," replied Lensky. "You cannot imagine what it is to play on an instrument which understands one. It is still only a little bit sleepy, but we will awaken it."

He placed a sonata of Beethoven before Natalie. They were alone. After the first bar of the nocturne the princess had fallen asleep, at the last she had waked, and had retired, with the remark that she could hear much better in the adjoining room.

"Will you really tolerate my accompaniment?" murmured the young girl.

"And do you wish to hear again, vain little princess, what I already told you in St. Petersburg, that I have seldom found a more sympathetic accompaniment than yours?" he replied.

She was an uncommonly good pianist, and with an unusually fine divination followed all the shades of his art. One piece followed the other. After awhile a certain relaxation was perceptible in her.

"You are tired," said he, breaking off in the middle of the first phrase of Mendelssohn's G-minor concerto. "I should not have given you so much to do. Pardon me."

"Oh, what does that matter," said she, while she let her hands slide from the keys. "It was splendid, only, do you see, I feel as if I am a dragging-shoe for you. I would like to have a wish, a great immoderate wish.　I would like to hear you once alone, without accompaniment, from your heart. Give me one glance into your soul, make your musical confession to me!"

He felt a peculiar twitching and burning in his finger-tips. He would rather have killed himself than let her glance into his inmost soul, as the condition of that soul had been until then.

" Do not ask that of me," said he, hoarse-ly.

" It was very immodest in me, excuse me," said she hastily and confused.

" Oh, that is nothing," he assured her. " Do you think that I will spare the little. bit of pleasure that I can perhaps give you, only—but if you really wish it—as far as I am concerned——"

He took up the violin.

It was a different affair now.　Dragging-shoe or not—in any case her accompaniment had had a calming and perhaps puri-fying effect on his musical instincts. With her he had played as a wonderfully deeply

sensitive and technically cultivated virtuoso; in spite of all the heartfelt fulness of
tone and vibrating passion, he had scarcely
passed the boundary of musical convention-
ality. It had been the highest possibility
of a quiet, artistic performance; but what
Natalie now heard was no longer art, but
something at once splendid and fearful. It
was also no longer a violin on which he
played, but a strange, enchanted instrument that she had never known formerly
and that he himself had invented; an instrument from which everything that sounds
the sweetest and saddest on earth vibrated,
from the low voice of a woman to the soft,
complaining sigh of the waves dying on the
shore. A depth of genial musical eloquence
burst forth under his bow. Inconsolable
pain—dry, hard, cutting; tender teasing,
winning grace, mad rejoicing, a wild confusion of passion and music, the height and
depth of neck-breaking technical extrava-
gance.

But what was most peculiar about his

playing, and had the most magical effect, was neither the mad **bravura nor the** flatter-ing grace, but something oppressive, mys-terious, that crept maliciously into the heart and veins, ensnaring and paralyzing—a thing of itself, a strange horror. Again and again, like a mysterious call, appeared in his im-provisation **the same bewitching, exciting succession of tones,** taken from the Ara-bian folk-songs, the devil's music.

Suddenly he seemed to be beside himself; he drew the bow across the violin as if beset by an untamable, passionate excitement. **It was no longer one violin which one heard; it was twenty violins, or,** rather, twenty demons, who howled and cried together.

With hands lightly folded in her lap, and head leaned back against her **chair,** Natalie had listened. In the beginning she had been carried out of herself by a feeling of painfully sweet happiness. But now she felt strangely oppressed. It seemed to her as if something pulled at every fibre, every nerve, as if her heart was bursting. She would have liked to cry out and hold her ears, and still did not move, but listened eagerly to that piercing, wild, passionate tone. Never had she felt within her such hot, beating, intense life as in this hour. Her whole past existence now seemed to her like a long, stupid lethargy, from which she had at last been awakened. Tears flowed from her eyes. Then his look met hers. A kind of shame at his brutality overcame him, and his playing died away in sad, sweet, anguished tenderness. With . contracted brows and trembling hands, he laid down the violin. "You wished it!" said he. "You should not have asked it of me. I can refuse you nothing. God! how pale you are! I have made you ill!"

She smiled at his anxious exaggeration, then murmured softly, as if in a dream: "It was wonderfully beautiful, and I shall never forget it—never forget it, only ——"

"What have you to object?"

"Shall I really tell you?"

"Certainly; I beg you to."

"Well," she began, hesitatingly, with a somewhat uneasy smile, as if she was afraid of wounding his irritable artistic sensibility, "I ask myself how one can abuse an instrument from which one can charm such bewitching harmonies, and which one loves as you love your violin, as you have just now abused it?"

He was silent for a moment, surprised, looked at the violin with a loving, compassionate glance, as if it were a living being. Then he passed his hand across his forehead.

"I do not know how it is," said he, confusedly. "Sometimes something comes over me. Ah! if you knew what it is to have, all one's life, such a sultry, sneaking thunderstorm in one's veins as I have. Sometimes it bursts forth; it must have vent. I cannot rule myself. Teach me how!"

He said that, so naïvely ashamed, quite pleadingly, like a great child; he had strangely warm, touching tones in his deep, rough voice.

.   .   .   .   .   .

When Lensky presented himself again,
the next day, in the Palazzo Morsini, and,
indeed, this time to arrange the purchase of
the wonderful violin, the princess called out
gayly to him:

"The violins are no longer to be had. I
have bought all three. I gave all my sav-
ings for them. If you wish to play on
them, you must come here. But—you
may come as often as you wish!"

"For how long?" asked he, with a peculiar tremble in his voice.

She turned away her head. After awhile
she said, apparently irrelevantly, with her
gay, ingenuous smile, that still never quite
banished the sadness from her pale face:
"Do you know that we are really as poor
as church mice? It is comical. Mamma
consoles herself with the thought that I
will make a good match. If she should be
mistaken, what a tragedy!"

She laughed merrily. What did she
mean by that?

.   .   .   .   .   .

He came oftener and oftener to the old palace in the Via Giulia; came every day, indeed.

Formerly intercourse with women of rank had always formed only a short parenthesis in his otherwise dissolute life. Now the couple of hours, or sometimes they were only minutes, which he daily passed with the Assanows were the key-note of all the rest of his existence. How happy he felt with them!

If elsewhere the great society ladies had raved over the artist Lensky to an immoderate extent, they had quite ignored the man. But with the Assanows it was different, or at least it seemed so. His fame was not put forward from morning to night. There were days in which his violin-playing was not even mentioned. The artist stopped in the background, and in association with Natalie and her mother he was no star, no lion, only a very wise, peculiar, sympathetic man, who pleased quite aside from his artistic gifts. Besides, with them he appeared differently than with any one else in the world.

His petulant defiance disappeared, as well as the helplessness for which it was a shield.

He was completely uncultivated from the foundation. Grown up among ignorant men who profited by his early unfolding talent, and misused it in order to earn money thereby; sentenced consequently as a child to just as many hours of hard musical practice as his poor still undeveloped body could endure, he had, at fourteen years of age, when he could barely read and write, not even the consciousness of his lack of knowledge. That came later, came when great people began to be interested in him. But then it was painful and humiliating beyond measure.

Whatever one can acquire in later years he acquired. Another would have made a show of the astonishing amount of reading which he had accomplished in the course of years, but he never learned to display his lately won intellectual riches with grace. He had not the frivolity of superficial men. Much too clever not to be conscious that his little bit of supplementary cultivation was still only patchwork, even if made of very noble, large patches, he confined his remarks in society, if the conversation was upon anything but music, to a few heavy commonplaces.

With Natalie and her mother it was quite different. He never, indeed, spoke very much, but everything that he said was characteristic, stimulating, interesting, and as, in spite of his sad lack of education, he was free from narrow provincialisms and af-fectations, and with the capability of assim-ilation of all barbarians, understood exactly Natalie's pure and poetic being, he never wounded her by a coarse lack of tact, but attracted her doubly by the austere uncon-ventionality of his manner.

Every day he became more sympathetic to her ; she had long been indispensable to him.

He was suddenly struck with horror of his past. It seemed to him as if everything that was beautiful in his life had just begun when her pure bright apparition had entered it. She had brought a cooling, healing element to his sultry existence. It was as if one had opened a window in a room full of oppressive vapor—a great breath of sweet, spicy air had purified the atmosphere.

A large part of his intellectual self which had formerly lain fallow, now grew and blossomed. Often, in the morning, he accompanied the ladies to some art collection. Very frequently he occupied a place in the carriage which the princess had hired for their drives.

Every one looked after the carriage, and observed with the same interest the wonderfully beautiful girl, and the great artist, who was not handsome, but whose face once seen could never be forgotten.

What was most remarkable about it was the difference between the expression of his eyes and that of his mouth, a difference which betrayed the entire quality of his inner nature. While his eyes had a spying, at times quite enthusiastic, expression, around the mouth was a trace of intense earthly thirst for enjoyment.

This mingling predestinated him to that eternal discontent of certain great natures who can just as little accustom themselves, on the earth, to a condition of bloodless asceticism as to one of mindless materialism. The first desires no enjoyment of the world, the second pleases itself with whatever is to be had in the world. Those men only who seek the heavenly spark in earthly joys remain forever deceived here. He was destined never to cease to seek it. Even in gray old age, when his finely cut lips were satiated with enjoyment, and were fixed in a grimace of incessant, sad disgust, his eyes still sought it.

.　　.　　.　　.　　.　　.

His colleagues in St. Petersburg asked each other what kept him so long in Rome.

He wrote one of them that he was working, and indeed he did work. Through his soul vibrated melodies full of bewitching sad loveliness, full of the rejoicing and complaint of a longing which could not yet attain the longed-for happiness.

And there in Rome, in those mild fragrant spring nights, he wrote a cyclus of songs which might rank at the side of the most beautiful musical lyrics ever written.

In spite of their full richness of melody, his earlier compositions had something too glaring, overladen, and trivially pleasing; they were too much influenced by his virtuosity to please for themselves. In his Roman cyclus of songs he showed himself for the first time a great musician. And as until then he had distrusted his talent as composer, he was pleasantly astonished over his own achievement.

He always worked at night. His writing-table stood in front of the window of his room which looked out on the Piazza di Spagna. Very often his glance wandered there. A dark-blue heaven lighted by thousands of stars arched above the broad, irregular place, over the antique columns, from whose height a modern art nonentity looks down on Rome.

All was silent, only the water, the resonant soul of Rome, tittered and sobbed in the basins and fountains, and spouted up jubilantly in damp silver streams, greeting from afar the unattainable heavens, and all the tittering, sobbing, and rejoicing united in a long vibrating broken chord.

Still vibrating in every fibre at the recollection of Natalie's farewell smile, he sat at his shaky table and wrote. The mild night wind, fragrant with the kisses which it had stolen from the magnolia and orange blossoms, crept in to him and caressed his hot cheeks. He inhaled it eagerly. He had often been warned of the Roman night air, but he did not think of the warning, and if he had—? He was in that happy mood in which man no longer believes in sickness and death.

The hateful melancholy which as he said often pressed him down to the ground, and tormented him with predictions of his final annihilation, was gone. He no longer saw, as formerly, an open grave at his feet. Heaven had opened to him. An indescribable, light, elevating feeling had overpowered him; he no longer felt the weight of his body. Had his wings, then, grown in Rome?

.   .   .   .   .   .

He did not think what would come of all this. He did not wish to think of it; did not wish to see clearly. With closed eyes he walked through life—the angels led him.

.   .   .   .   .   .

It was the beginning of May, and he had finished his cyclus of songs. With a beating heart he entered the Palazzo Morsini to ask Natalie whether he might dedicate it to her.

The young princess was not at home, but her mother would be very happy to see him, they told him.

It was very hot, the blinds were all lowered. The princess lay on a lounge and
fanned herself with a peacock feather fan.

After she had complained of the heat,
she began to speak to him of all kinds of
family affairs. Her son had the best of
opportunities to make a career for himself,
said she; her eldest daughter, who was far
less pretty than Natalie, added the princess,
had married very well; her husband was
indeed a wealthy diplomat. "*Mois, je suis
pauvre,*" concluded the old lady; "but I
could live quite without care, if Natalie were
only married. But she will hear nothing
of that. She lets the best years of her life
pass, and if you only knew what good
matches she has refused. Pachotin has
already offered himself twice to her, and if
you please——"

Just then a gay voice interrupted the
inconsolable elegy. "Mamma, how can
any one boast so?" Natalie had entered,
a large black hat on her head, in her arms a
huge bunch of flowers.

" I did not boast—I complained," replied the old woman, sighing.

After Natalie had greeted Lensky with her usual friendliness, she laid the flowers on the table and arranged them in the vases which an Italian chambermaid had brought her.

" Ah, Natalie, why will you have none of them?" sighed the princess.

" Little mother, I can love but once," replied Natalie, bending her brown head over the flowers. " I have told you I will not marry until I have found some one quite extraordinary—a hero or a genius."

" Am I dreaming, or did she look at me with those words?" Lensky asked himself. " But why did she turn her eyes away so quickly when they met mine?"

Meanwhile the princess said : " Yes, if all girls wished to wait thus!"

" I am not like all girls," said Natalie, laughing. " Most girls have hearts like hand-organs, which every one can play ; others have hearts like Æolian harps, on which

4

no one can play, and still they always
vibrate so sympathetically for the world;
and still other girls—" she interrupted
herself to break a superfluous leaf from a
magnolia twig.

The princess, who seemed to lay little
weight on Natalie's naïve comparisons,
fanned herself indifferently with her peacock fan, but Lensky repeated, "Well,
Natalie Alexandrovna, other girls——"

"Other girls have hearts like Amati violins; if a bungler touches them there is a
horrible discord; but if a true artist comes
who understands it, then——"

This exaggerated remark she had made
in a voice trembling between mockery and
tenderness, and incessantly occupied with
the arrangement of her flowers.

Without ending the last sentence, she
broke off, and bent her head to the right to
observe a combination of white roses and
heliotrope with a thoughtful look.

The princess yawned from heat and discontent. "Leave me in peace from your

musical comparisons, Natascha," said she.
" Besides, I can assure you that no one
spoils a fine instrument quicker than one of
your great virtuosos. When I think how
Franz Liszt ruined our Pleyel in a single
evening; it was no longer fit even for a
conservatory."

" Violins are not ruined as quickly as
pianos," said Natalie, laughing; then, still
speaking to the flowers, she said: " Don't
you think, little mother, that if such a piano
had a soul, a mind, it would rather rejoice to
really live for once under the hands of a
great master, and even if it were to die of
the joy, than merely to exist for a half-century in a noble, charming room, as a carefully preserved showpiece?"

Again it seemed to Lensky that she
looked at him, and again she turned away
her head when their looks met. " You are
astonished at this great expenditure for
flowers?" she remarked. " We expect
guests this evening—my cousins from St.
Petersburg, the Jeliagins. You know them,

and I shall try to draw their critical looks away from the holes in the furniture covering to these beautiful color effects. So! Now I have finished; here are a few May-bells left for your button-hole. Ah! really, you never wear flowers!"

"Give them to me," said he, contracting his brows gloomily. She smiled at him without saying anything. Then something scratched at the door.

"Please open it, Boris Nikolaivitch," she asked.

He did so; her large dog, a gigantic Scotch greyhound, came in, and immediately springing up on his beautiful mistress, he laid both front paws on her shoulders. She took his heavy head between her slender hands, and murmuring tender, caressing words to him, she kissed him twice, three times, on the forehead.

Lensky took leave soon after without having mentioned his song cyclus. His mind was in an uproar. "Is she only coquetting with me?" he asked himself, "or—

or—" A passionate joy throbbed in his veins, then suddenly an icy shudder ran over him. "And if she is only like all the others!"

At his departure Natalie had said to him: "You will come this evening, Boris Niko- laivitch, in spite of this boring Petersburg invasion? I beg you will, *vous serez le coin bleu de mon ciel!*"

.   .   .   .   .   .

The evening came.

A Roman sirocco evening, with an ap- proaching thunderstorm that hung heavily around the horizon and would not lift.

The heavily perfumed sultry air pene- trated through the drawn curtains into the Assanows' drawing-room. The Jeliagins had brought a couple of Parisian friends with them, and naturally Pachotin was not missing. A deathly *ennui* reigned. They spoke of Parisian fashions, of the Empress Eugenie's new court; they complained of the new cook in the Hotel de l'Europe, and of the heat.

Then they spoke of national dances. The Jeliagins had recently travelled in Spain and were enthusiastic about the fandango. The Parisians had heard there was nothing more graceful than a well-danced Polish mazurka; could none of the Russian ladies dance one for them?—a very bold request, but they were all friends.

The Jeliagins announced that Natalie danced the mazurka like a true woman of Warsaw. They left her no peace.

"Oh, I will put on no more airs," said she, "if one of the ladies will take a seat at the piano, so———"

To go to the piano, even were it only to play dance-music, in Lensky's presence! The ladies swooned at the mere thought.

"Very well, then you must give up the mazurka," said Natalie, decidedly.

"Ask Boris Nikolaivitch," whispered one of the St. Petersburg women. "If he is the first violinist of his time, he is also an excellent pianist."

"No, no," said Natalie, firmly, and then her great brilliant eyes met Lensky's.

Although at that time he maintained his artistic dignity with quite childish exaggeration, he smiled very good-naturedly and said, "I see very well that you place no confidence in me; you think I cannot catch your mazurka music."

"No, no, no!" said Natalie. "You shall not degrade your art."

"And do you really think it would be degrading to improvise a musical background for your performance? I should so like to see you dance." And he stood up and went to the piano.

Such pretty little phrases were formerly not his style. He had, as Natalie had often laughingly told him, no talent for *fioriture* in conversation.

The Petersburg ladies looked at each other. "How polite he has become! You have changed him, Natascha," whispered they.

Meanwhile Pachotin gave Natalie his hand.

Lensky had seized the opportunity of admiring her grace with joy. He had never thought how painfully it would affect him to see her dance with another man. He did not take his eyes off her, and meanwhile improvised the most bewitching devil's music.

She wore a white dress, her neck and arms were bare, and around her waist was a Circassian girdle embroidered with gold and silver. One hand in her partner's, the other hanging loosely at her side, her head slightly on one side, she moved safely over the dangerously smooth surface of the marble floor. At the beginning, pale as usual, except her dark-red lips, she looked quite indifferent ; gradually she became warmer and more animated, a slight blush crept into her cheeks, her eyes beamed as if in a happy dream, around her lips trembled the sad expression which the feeling of intense pleasure often causes us, and her movements at the same time had something indescribably gentle and supple.

AT THE BEGINNING, PALE AS USUAL, EXCEPT THE DARK-RED LIPS, SHE LOOKED QUITE INDIFFERENT; GRADUALLY SHE BECAME WARMER AND MORE ANIMATED, A SLIGHT BLUSH CREPT INTO HER CHEEKS, HER EYES BEAMED AS IN A HAPPY DREAM—

p. 56.

Pachotin, most correctly attired, with a collar which reached to the tips of his ears and faultless yellow gloves, hopped around her in the true affected knightly grimacing Polish-mazurka manner.

"An ape!" thought Lensky to himself; "but how handsome, how distinguished he is! almost as handsome as she!" and suddenly the question occurred to him: "Is it my music or his presence which animates her? And if it were my music! Nevertheless, she will still marry him; yes, even if she were in love with me, still she would marry him, and not me! What a fool I was to imagine——"

After Pachotin had soberly placed his heels together and acknowledged his deep devotion to the lady by a suitable courtesy, the mazurka was at an end.

Quite beside themselves with enthusiasm, the Parisians surrounded Natalie. When she wished to thank Lensky he had disappeared. It was his manner many times to withdraw without taking leave, but still to-day it made Natalie uneasy. She was vibrating with a great excitement, the air seemed to her suffocatingly hot, she drew off her gloves: the noise of the prattling voices became unbearable to her, and she passed through the second empty drawing-room, into the arched loggia set with blooming orange-trees, from which one looked across the court-yard to the Tiber.

The storm still hung on the horizon. Heavy masses of clouds, shot through by pale lightning, towered, on the other side of the river, above the gloomy architecture of the Trastevere. They had not yet reached the moon, which, palely shining, stood high in the heavens. Its light illumined the court, with its statues and bas-reliefs. The air was sultry.

Natalie drew a deep breath. Suddenly she discovered Lensky. He was staring down on the Tiber, which, rolling by in its bed, incessantly sighed, as if from sorrow at its sad lot, which compelled it continually to hasten past everything.

Could one really take it amiss in the stream if it sometimes overflowed its banks in order to carry away with it some of the beautiful objects, near which, condemned to perpetual wandering, it might not remain standing?

"Ah! you here?" said Natalie. "I thought you had taken French leave. I was vexed with you."

"So!"

"Yes, because—because I was sorry not to be able to thank you. It was really——"

"Do not speak so," said he, quite rough-ly; "just as if you did not know that there is nothing in the world, nothing in my power that I would not do for you!"

She bent her head back a little and smiled at him in a friendly way, but as if his words had not surprised her in the slightest. "You are very good to me," said she.

He felt strangely thus alone with her in this sweet-perfumed, melancholy, intoxicat-ing sultriness, alone with this happiness that was so near him, and which he was afraid of frightening away by an unseemly imprudence. He felt by turns **hot and cold.** Why did she not go?

She rested her hands on the marble balustrade of the loggia and bending over it she murmured: " How beautiful ! oh, how wonderfully beautiful ! And it is so tiresome in there ; do you not find it so, Boris Nikolaivitch ?"

His throat contracted, he felt that he was about to lose control of himself.

" Shall I play?" he asked. " I will do it willingly for you."

" Oh, no ! Why should you play to those stupid people in there?" replied she. " I would be prepared to hear, in the middle of the G minor concerto, the question : ' Before I forget it, can you not give me the address of a good shoemaker in Rome?' You know how such things vex me."

" Is she coquetting with me, or—?" he asked himself again.

She stood before him with her enchant-

"OH, YOU DEAR, DEAR GIRL!" HE MURMURED, WITH HOARSE, SCARCELY AUDIBLE VOICE, AND PRESSED IT TO HIS LIPS.

CRIMSONING, SHE TORE AWAY HER HAND.

p. 61.

ing face, and her tender glance met his. She did not know that she tormented him. In spite of her twenty-one years, she had the boundless innocence of a girl whose mind has never been desecrated by the knowledge of passion, a degree of innocence in which men do not believe.

"Is she coquetting?" His heart beat to bursting, and suddenly, when she quite unconstrainedly came one step nearer him, he took her hand. "Oh, you dear, dear girl!" he murmured, with hoarse, scarcely audible voice, and pressed it to his lips.

Crimsoning, she tore away her hand. "For Heaven's sake, what are you thinking of?" said she, and started back with a proud, almost scornful gesture.

Then a horrible anger overcame him.

"I was stupid, I was mistaken in you. You think no more nobly or better than the others!" he burst out.

"I do not understand you. What do you mean?" murmured she.

What else had she to ask? Why did she

not go, but stood before him, as if par-
alyzed, with her pale, seductive loveliness,
surrounded by moonlight?

"I mean that if you observe our relations from this conventional standpoint,
your behavior to me was a heartless, arrogant abomination."

"But, Boris Nikolaivitch, that is all
foolishness. You do not know what you
are saying," she stammered, quite beside
herself.

"So! I do not know what I am saying?"
He had now stepped close up to her. "And
if I, mistaking your coquetries—yes, that
is the word; blush now and be a little
ashamed—if I, mistaking your coquetries,
have permitted myself to petition for your
hand? Oh, how you start! Naturally, you
had never thought of such a thing!"

His voice was hoarse and rasping, his face
very calm and as if petrified by anger and
such a mental torment as he had never before experienced. "But go! Why do you
stay and torture me? I will no longer look

at you. I abominate you, and still I love you so passionately, so madly!"

Yes, why did she still not go? He could endure it no longer—he clasped her to his breast and kissed her with his hot, burning lips. Then she pushed him from her and fled.

He looked after her. Now all was over. For one moment he remained standing on the same spot, then, with deeply bowed head, dragging his feet along slowly, he passed through the vestibule and left, without thinking of his hat, which he had left in the drawing-room.

For the remainder of the evening Natalie's whole being betrayed only haste and uneasiness. She spoke more and quicker than formerly, laughed frequently, and told the gayest stories.

When her Petersburg cousins wished to tease her with Lensky's enthusiasm for her, and laughingly called him " your genius," she mentioned him indifferently, quite disapprovingly, shrugged her shoulders over

his talent as composer—yes, even found
fault with his playing. She was friendly,
quite inviting, to Pachotin; she no longer
knew what she did, only when he wished
to give the conversation a more earnest
turn she broke it off suddenly and remorse-
lessly.

When at last, at last, the drawing-room
was empty and she might withdraw, she
locked herself in her room, threw herself
down before the holy picture before which
she always said her evening prayer. But,
however she tried to pray, she could not.
She did not know for what she should pray.
Her cheeks burned with dreadful shame.
How could he have so far forgotten himself
with her!

She threw open a window. What did it
matter to her that they said the Roman
night air was poisonous? She would have
liked to take the Roman fever, would have
liked to die. Her window opened on the
street. The Via Giulia was divided by the
moonlight into two parts, one light and one

dark. All was quiet, empty, deserted. Then there was a sound of slow, dragging steps, and two lowered voices whispered down there in the silent solitude. It was probably a pair of belated lovers, and suddenly there was a soft, tender sound through the mild May night. She caught her breath, closed the window, and turned back to her room. Half-undressed, she sat on the edge of her little cool white bed and thought again and again—of the same thing—of his kiss.

.   .   .   .   .   .

"Why has 'your genius' so suddenly tired of Rome? He leaves to-day," remarked the Jeliagins, who had come to lunch the next morning in the Palazzo Morsini.

They were staying at the same hotel as Lensky—that is to say, in the "Europe"—and had spoken to him in the court of the hotel. "He looked miserably," they added, with a haughty glance. "Either he has Roman fever or you have broken his heart."

Then they spoke of other things. Soon after lunch they went away.

Meanwhile Lensky stumbled up and down, up and down, in his room. A sick lady whose room was beneath his, at last sent up by the waiter and begged him to be quiet.

His departure was fixed for seven o'clock; it struck one, it struck four.

Should he leave without having made a parting call upon the Princess Assanow—run away like any fellow who has borrowed thirty rubles? "But they will not receive me," he thought, "if the princess has told her mother. But, no, she will have said nothing; she is too proud. What a lovely being! How could I only— Oh, if I might at least ask her pardon! But what kind of a pardon would it be? Such a thing a woman pardons only if she loves, and how should she love me, a beast as I am? She must have an aversion for me."

He resolved to take leave by letter. He tried it in French and Russian, but could complete nothing. Ashamed of his laughable incapacity, he tore up the different sheets of letter-paper adorned with " *Des circonstances imprévues,*" or " *La reconnaissance sincère que.*"

Five o'clock! He hastened across the courtyard, sprang into a carriage. " Palazzo Morsini, Via Giulia," he called to the coachman, and commanded him to drive fast.

When he ascended the well-known stairs he asked himself a last time if he would be received.

The servant conducted him to the boudoir of the old princess. She broke off her game of patience to greet him, only betrayed a slight astonishment at his sudden departure, and said that she and Natalie should soon follow his example and go North, probably to Baden-Baden, for the heat in Rome began to be unbearable. Then she rang for the maid, whom she commissioned to tell the princess that Boris Nikolaivitch had come to take leave.

Lensky waited in breathless excitement.

The maid came back with the decision : The princess was very ill and had lain down with a headache.

"Quite as I expected," thought Lensky, while the princess remarked politely, " She will be very sorry."

Then he kissed the old lady's hand, she touched his forehead with her lips in the Russian custom, wished him a pleasant journey, he thanked her a last time for all the friendship she had shown him, and went —went quite slowly through the large empty room, in which the dust danced in a broad sunbeam which lay across the marble floor, and in which the flowers which she had arranged so charmingly yesterday now stood withered in their vases.

"Shall I never see her again, never— never?" he asked himself. He would have given his life for a last friendly glance from her. What use was it to think of that—it was all over !

Then suddenly he heard something near him like the rustling of an angel's wings.

He looked up. Natalie stood before him, deathly pale, with black rings around her eyes, with carelessly arranged hair. A passionate pity, a tender anxiety overcame him. " How she has suffered through my offence ! " he told himself, and rushed up to her. " Natalie, can you forgive me ? " he called.

Her great, sad eyes were raised to him with an expression of helpless, ashamed tenderness, as if they would say, " And you ask that ! " She moved her lips, but no word came.

He held her little hands trembling with fever in his. She did not draw them away. He grew dizzy. For one moment they were both silent, then he whispered, drawing her closer to him, " Do you love me, then ? Could you resolve to bear my name, to share my whole existence ? "

Scarcely audibly she whispered, " Yes."

We are sometimes frightened at the sudden fulfilment of a wish which we have believed unattainable.

And as Lensky under the weight of his
new, strange happiness sank at the feet of
his betrothed and covered the hem of her
dress with tears and kisses, in the midst of
his happiness he felt an oppressed anxiety,
a great fear.

.   .   .   .   .   .

A few days after Natalie's betrothal there
was a short, imperious ring at the door of
the artistic gray anteroom, in which the
imposing butler, as usual, sat majestically
intrenched behind his newspaper.

Monsieur Baptiste raised his eyebrows;
he did not like this imperious manner of
ringing a bell, and did not hurry at all to
open the door. Only when the ring was repeated did he unlock it. His face changed
color from surprise, and he bowed quite to
the ground when he recognized in the entering gentleman the young prince, the
eldest brother of Natalie, Sergei Alexandrovitch Assanow.

"Are the ladies at home?" he asked
shortly in a high, somewhat vexed voice

without further noticing the respectful greeting of the servant.

" The princess is still in bed, but the Princess Natalie is already up."

" Good. Do not disturb the princess, and announce me to Princess Natalie," said Assanow, and with that he followed the butler, who was hastening before him, into the drawing-room. There he sat down in a mahogany arm-chair upholstered in faded yellow damask, crossed his legs, rested his tall shining hat on his knee and looked around him. On one of his hands was a gray glove, the other was bare. It was a long, slender, aristocratic hand, very well cared for, too white for a man's hand, but bony, and with strongly marked veins on the back—a hand which one saw would certainly hold firmly what it had once grasped, and a hand which was capable of no caress. For the rest it would have been hard to judge anything from the exterior of the prince. He was a tall slender man of about thirty, with light-brown hair that was already thin on the top of the head, and a face—smoothly shaven except a long mustache—which in the cut of the delicate regular features resembled his sister's not unnoticeably. But the expression, that animating soul of beauty which lent Natalie's pale face more charm than the regularity of the lines, was lacking in him. Everything about him was as correct as his profile—his high stiff collar, the drab gaiters which showed beneath his trousers, his light-gray gloves with black stitching. He was the type of the Russian state official of the highest category, the type of men who in public life only permit themselves to think as far ·as will not injure their advancement.

As he was a very clever, sharp, judging man withal, he revenged himself for the discomfort which the systematic crippling of his intellectual capacity in the service of the state caused him, by devoting all the superfluity of his unneeded intellect to shedding an unpleasantly glaring intellectual light about him, and condemning as absolute foolishness all those little poetic, pleasant trifles which make life beautiful.

He called this manner of pleasing himself doing his duty.

Strangely enough, with all his sterile dryness he was a true lover of music. He played the 'cello as well as a man of the world can permit himself to—that is to say, with an elegant inaccuracy, together with pedantic bursts of virtuosity, and in consequence had cultivated Lensky's acquaintance assiduously.

While he waited for his sister he looked around the room distrustfully with his handsome dark but unpleasantly piercing eyes. He grew uneasy. The atmosphere of the whole room was quite permeated with happiness. Everything seemed to feel happy here—the shabby furniture, the music which lay somewhat confusedly on the piano. On the table near which Sergei Alexandrovitch sat stood a basket of pale Malmaison roses, under the piano was a violin case.

Sergei Alexandrovitch frowned. Then Natalie entered the room ; he rose, went to meet her, kissed and embraced her. It seemed strange to her that she did not feel as glad to see him as formerly, but rather felt a kind of chill. Which of them had changed, he or she?

" What a surprise ! " said she, and felt herself that her voice had a forced sound. " It has **not** formerly been your custom to appear so unexpectedly."

" My journey was only decided upon last month," replied he, somewhat hesitatingly; and with his dull smile he added, " I hope I do not arrive inopportunely, Natalie?"

" How can you ask such a thing ! " said she. " But sit down and put your hat away—you are at home."

He remarked the uneasiness of her manner. He coughed twice, and then sat down again near the table on which the basket of roses stood.

Natalie sat down. Both hands resting on the red surface of the mahogany table,

she bent over the flowers, and slowly with
a kind of tenderness inhaled the dreamy,
melancholy perfume.

"Have you had a pleasant winter?" began Sergei Alexandrovitch.

"I do not know," replied she without
looking at him; "I have forgotten, but the
spring was wonderfully beautiful, wonderfully beautiful," and she bent over the
flowers again.

"Hm! So you prefer Rome to Naples?"
said he condescendingly.

"Yes."

"You seem to have been very comfortably fixed here," he remarked, with a glance
around. "You have very pretty rooms.
Those are beautiful roses which you have
there."

"Boris Lensky sent them to me," said
she, while she at the same time pulled a
rose from the basket to fasten it in the
bodice of her light foulard dress. Then she
sat down opposite Sergei. War was declared.

"Lensky seems to be a great deal with you," said Assanow, condescendingly.

"Yes."

"I heard of it through acquaintances in Petersburg," began the prince. "It did not quite please me."

Natalie only shrugged her shoulders, with an expression as if she would say: "I am very sorry, but that does not change matters at all." In spite of that she secretly trembled before her brother. The announcement which she had to make to him would not cross her lips.

"It is hard to speak of certain things to you," he continued, while he tried to make his thin high voice sound confidential. He did not wish to make his sister refractory by overhasty roughness. "I have no prejudices." It had recently become the fashion in his set, and especially for the upper ten thousand, to boast of a kind of harmless liberality. "No one can accuse me of smallness. I am always in favor of attracting young artists into society—first,

because they form an animating element in
our circles, and secondly, because one should
give them an opportunity to improve their
manners a little; but all in moderation.
Too great intimacy in such cases is bad for
both parties. You are too much carried
away by the generosity of your heart. I
know that in reality your immoderate
kindness to Lensky does not mean much,
but——"

Her wonderfully beautiful eyes met
his.

" I am betrothed to Boris Nikolaivitch,"
said she wearily but very distinctly.

" Betrothed!" he burst out. "You to
Lensky? You are crazy!"

" Not at all."

" Does mother know of it?"

" Certainly."

" And she has given her consent?"

"At first she was surprised; she cried a
whole afternoon. I was very sorry to pain
her. Then she gave way. She is very fond
of him. Every one must be fond of him

who learns to know him well." Natalie's
eyes beamed with animation.

Sergei Alexandrovitch pulled at his mustache. " Hm, hm," he murmured ; " we
will leave that undecided. As it happens, I
am one of those who know him well ; there
are few in our set who know him as intimately as I, and—hm—I do not know that
he has caused me any very enthusiastic
feelings. As artist I rank him very high,
not so high as has been the fashion lately,
for as a *beau dire il manque de style*, he
lacks style ! But that has nothing to do
with this. But if he united in himself the
genius of Beethoven and Paganini, I would
still look upon the possibility of your alliance with him as unheard of, and I tell you
frankly, that I shall do all that is in my
power to prevent it." He had taken up
again the hat which he had formerly laid
down, and held it on his knee as if paying
a call of state. While he spoke the last
words, he knocked on the top of it with
malicious decision.

Natalie crossed her arms.

" I knew that you would oppose the mésalliance," said she, " but——"

He would not let her finish. " Mésalliance ! " said he, and laughed very mockingly, quite shortly and softly, to himself, and
began to drum on the top of his hat again.
" Mésalliance ! I cannot say that the marriage of my sister to this Mr. Lensky would
be especially pleasant—no, that I cannot
say. What must be my horror at your
undertaking if I scarcely think of my opposition on account of the unequal birth ! "
He was silent, but then as Natalie remained
obstinately silent, he continued : " That
you will in consequence change your social
position is your affair. But do not believe
that this will be all that you give up. You
sacrifice not only your position, your whole
personality, all your habits of life, but more
than all these, you sacrifice all your formerly
so spared and guarded womanly tender feeling if you insist upon marrying this violinist.
Oh, I know what you will say," said he,

while he noticed the glance which Natalie
gave the roses on the table. " He is full of
poetic attentions for you. When they are
in love, the roughest men speak in verse.
And I believe that he loves you. But his
enthusiasm for you is still only a passing
effervescence. What will remain when that
is gone? I ask you, what would remain in
a man without principles, without a trace of
moral restraint, who has · grown up amid
surroundings which have forever blunted
his feelings for things which would horrify
you, and others of which you have no suspicion ? "

Again he paused, · but this time Natalie
spoke : " May I ask you," began she, with
the calm behind which irritation bordering
on uncontrollable anger concealed itself—
" may I ask you to tell me exactly, without
any more finely veiled insinuations, what
you have against Boris Nikolaivitch, except
that he is of lower birth and has enjoyed
no careful bringing up ? "

" My God ! If it is a question of my sister's future husband, that is enough and more than enough!" said Assanow.

"Is it all?" asked Natalie, and looked at him penetratingly.

"What do you mean?"

"Is it all?" she repeated, while she slowly rose from her chair. "Have you anything else against him?"

"I have really nothing against him as long as it is not a question of my sister's husband," he hissed; "but in that case everything. And if instead of Lensky he were called Prince Dolgorouki, I would still say, as a husband for you he is impossible!"

"Why—I wish to know it—why?"

"Why? Good. I will tell you, as far as one can tell you—because he is a wild animal, with bursts of roughness of which you cannot form the slightest conception," said Assanow; and, striking his thin hands together, he added, with evidently genuine excitement: "*Mais, ma pauvre fille*, you have no suspicion to what humiliations, what degradations, you expose yourself."

He stopped. He looked at his sister triumphantly. She still stood before him with her hand resting on the top of the table, staring, pale and without a word. It would be false to say that his speech made no impression on her. It had made an impression on her. Still, she ascribed all that he said to boundless, passionate opposition. While he spoke it seemed to her as if little pointed icicles were hurled in her face. And weary and wounded from this hail-storm of fruitless prudence, she longed with all her heart for a reconciling delusion.

He misunderstood her apparently great excitement, and in the firm conviction that she already secretly began to fall in with his opinion, he began, this time in a kindly, playful tone: "My poor Natalie, my poor, unwise but always charming sister, you are like children who see that they are wrong and are ashamed to acknowledge it. Well, we will not press you too much. At first it is always painful to be undeceived; but time cures everything, and when you are married to a distinguished and reasonable young fellow—*un garçon distingué et raisonnable*—who will rationally cure you of your romantic ideas, you will only think of this youthful foolishness with a smile."

She threw back her head and measured him from head to foot. At this moment he seemed to her quite pitiable. How poverty-stricken, how sad was his whole inner life, his feelings, his thoughts, to those to which she had recently accustomed herself! "And you really believe that it could occur to me to give up Boris Nikolaivitch?" said she slowly with proudly curved lips.

"I think, after what I have said to you—" He tried to be patient, and even wished to take her hand, but she drew it back; the touch of his cold, bloodless fingers was unpleasant to her. Yet it had never been so before. What had changed in her?

The prince's face took on a hard, vexed expression. "I think after what I have told you—" he repeated.

"Is it not true, after what you have told me, after the consolation you have offered me, you cannot understand that I keep my word?" said she, challengingly. "What will you, I am now so foolish?" Her voice, veiled at first, became warmer and stronger, while she continued: "You take away summer from me, and offer me winter as consolation—that is, you ask of me that I should refuse everything in the world that blooms and bears fruit, only because sometimes a devastating thunderstorm bursts over this wealth of beauty and life! I know that in a normal winter there are no thunderstorms, and in spite of that I prefer the summer!"

"But it is a tropical summer!" exclaimed Assanow.

"That may be," she replied, calmly; "but for that very reason it is more magnificent—yes, even because of the dangers involved in it—more magnificent than any other."

He stood up. "It is useless to speak to

you," said he, coldly; " the only thing that remains for me is to speak to Lensky. He has a clear head in spite of all his genius. He can be talked over."

Then Natalie was startled out of her proud calm. "You would be indelicate enough to say to him what you have said to me!" she burst out.

" In such cases it is not only wisest, but most humane, to use pure prudence instead of foolish sentimentality," announced Assanow; and, bowing to his sister as to a stranger, he left, with all his vexation, still elevated by the thought that he had again had opportunity to display his " prudence " in a brilliant light. He loved his prudence as an artistic capability, and was glad to give proofs, by all kinds of virtuoso performances, of its extent and unusual pliability. Whether these productions were exactly suited to the time troubled the virtuoso little, and that by his last threat he had attained exactly the opposite with Natalie from what he wished, did not occur to him at all, momentarily.

He had gone. Natalie still stood in the
middle of the room, her hand resting on
the table, and trembling in her whole body.
Suddenly the memory of the "musical confession" arose in her, which Lensky had
laid before her the morning when he tried
the Amati, the confession which had frightened her. And through her mind vibrated,
piercingly and cuttingly, the mysterious
succession of tones from the Arabian folk-
songs which echoed lamentingly through
all his compositions—the devil's music:
Asbeïn.

As long as she had to defend herself from
her brother, she had not realized how
deeply he had wounded her. She felt at
once miserable, wounded, and discontented
with life—as a young tree must feel, over
whose fragrant young spring blossoms a hail-
storm has passed. Then Lensky came in.
He perceived in a moment what had happened..

"They have tormented you on my account," said he. "Poor heart! if I could

only take all this vexation upon my-self."

She smiled at him. "Then I would not be worthy of you," replied she.

He drew her gently toward him. Her discouragement had disappeared; warm, strong life again pulsated in her veins.

"Everything has its recompense," whispered she; "it is sweet to bear something for any one whom——"

"Well, for any one whom—please finish," he urged, and drew her closer to him.

"You know it without."

"I would so love to hear you say it once."

She raised herself on tiptoes and whispered something in his ear.

He held her tighter and tighter to him. "Oh, my happiness, my queen!" he murmured, and his warm lips met hers.

She felt as if wrapped in a sunbeam, in a warm, animating atmosphere, through which none of the critical sneers and opinions of those who stood without the consecrated magic circle of love could penetrate.

.   .   .   .   .   .

Six weeks later Natalie and Lensky were married, and at the Russian Embassy in Vienna. Her dowry consisted of a very incomplete trousseau, in part lavishly trimmed with lace ; of a mortgaged estate in South Russia that had brought in no rents for three years ; and of three Cremona violins.

While her elder brother silently concealed the true despair which the marriage caused him behind stiff dignity, the younger, an officer of the guard, with a becoming talent for arrogant impertinences, pleased himself by jesting over this adventurous marriage, and describing the " strange taste " of his sister, with a shrug of the shoulders, as a case of acute monomania. When he spoke of his brother-in-law, he called him nothing but " *cette bête sauvage et indécrottable,*" even when he had long made a practice of borrowing money of him.

Neither of Natalie's brothers or her married sister appeared at her wedding. Only the old princess accompanied her daughter to the altar.

SECOND BOOK.

THEY trifled away the summer on the Italian coast and in Switzerland. In the autumn Lensky made a concert tour through Germany and the Netherlands, on which his young wife accompanied him, and attempted with humorous zeal to accustom herself to the role of an artist's wife. In the beginning of December Lensky and she came to St. Petersburg. The residence had been prepared for the young pair by a friend of Natalie. Natalie made a discontented face when she entered her new kingdom. How new, how glaring, how unsuitable and tasteless everything looked. "It is as if one bit into a green apple," said she; and turning to Lensky she added, gayly, with a shrug of her shoulders: "The stupid Annette did not know any better; but do

not trouble yourself. In a couple of weeks
it will be different. You shall see how comfortably I will cushion your nest. You
must feel happy in it, my restless eagle, or
else you will fly away from me. What?"

She said this, smiling in proud consciousness of his passionate love. What pleasure
would it give him to fly away? And teas-
ingly, jestingly, she pushed back the thick
hair from his temples.

Ah, how pleasant and yet tantalizing was
the touch of her slender, delicate fingers,
which made him at once nervous and
happy! As he expressed it, it "almost
made him jump out of his skin with rapture." At first he let her continue her
foolish, tender playfulness to her heart's
content; then he laughingly put himself
on the defensive, preached a more digni-
fied manner to her, and when she did
not yield, but gayly continued her lovely,
teasing ways, he at length seized her violently by both wrists and quite crushed her
hands with kisses.

If in the first weeks of their married life both had been quite solemn, thoughtful, and confused in their manner to each other, now they often frolicked together like two gay children.

While he took up again his long-interrupted duties at the Petersburg Conservatory, she built him "his nest." She did not go lavishly to work. Oh, no! She knew that one must not press down a young artist with the burden of material cares. She imagined she was very economical. She did not cease to wonder over the cheapness with which she could get everything that was needed, beginning with the flowers—flowers in winter, in St. Petersburg! He never enlightened her as to how much the footing on which she maintained her "simple household" surpassed his present circumstances.

Every time that he came home he found a new, attractive change. She accomplished great things in artistic arrangement of the so-called "confused style," which at that

time was not so common as to-day, but was
still a bold innovation.

"*C'est très joli, mais un peu trop touffu,*"
said he to her once when she met him, quite
particularly conscious of victory and await-
ing praise, with the knowledge of a new,
costly improvement in the arrangement of
the drawing-room.

"Yes, my love; but a drawing-room is
neither an official audience-room nor a gym-
nasium," replied she, somewhat offended.

"Nor a ball-room nor riding-school," completed he, jestingly; "but—h'm—still one
should be able to move in it. Do you not
think so?"

"That is as one looks at it. I have nothing to do with it if you cannot brandish
around too freely in it."

.   .   .   .   .   .

They went out in society quite frequently
—in Natalie's society. That many people,
especially Natalie's near relations, made
comments on the marriage of the spoiled
child of a prince with a violinist is easily

understood. But scarcely had they seen Boris and his young wife together a few times when the comments ceased. A full, true, young human happiness always causes respect, and, like every achievement, bears its triumphant justification in itself. The leader of fashion, Princess Lydia Petrovna B., declared publicly, and, indeed, in the highest court circles, that in her opinion Natalie had acted very wisely.

Countess Sophie Dimitrievna went a step further when she energetically declared that she envied Natalie. From that time every one vied in fêting the young couple and distinguishing them.

They both enjoyed society, but the best part of it was not entering the brilliantly illuminated reception-rooms or being surrounded by wondering strangers. Oh, no! the best of all was the last quarter of an hour before they left their home, when Lensky, already in evening dress, entered the dressing-room of his young wife. Each time he felt anew the same pleasant excitement when he, slowly turning the knob, after a teasing, " May I come in, Natalie ?" entered the cosey room. How charming and attractive everything was there ! The room with the light carpet and the comfortable, not too numerous articles of cretonne-up-holstered furniture; the two tiny gold-em-broidered slippers on the rough bear-skin in front of the lounge; not far off, Natalie's house-dress, thrown over a chair, exhaling the warmth of her young, fresh, fragrant personality. Then there on the toilet-table, with clouds of white muslin over the pink lining, and with sparkling silver and crystal utensils, a pretty confusion of half-opened white lace boxes, and on the table dark velvet jewel-cases. The pleasant, mild, and still bright light of many pink wax-candles, which stood about in high, heavy silver candelabra, and the warm, strange, seduc-tive atmosphere which filled the whole room—an atmosphere which was permeated with the fragrance of greenhouse flowers, burning wax-candles, and the pleasant, subtle, spicy Indian perfume which clung to all Natalie's effects.

And there, before the tall cheval-glass, Natalie, already in evening toilet, almost ready, her beautiful arms hanging down in pampered helplessness; behind her a maid, just finished fastening her corsage, and a second, with a three-branched candelabra in her hand, throwing the light upon her mistress.

Was that really his wife? This splendid, queenly being in the white silk dress—she wore white silk in preference—really the wife of the violinist, in whose life, not so far back, lay all kind of need, humiliation, trouble of all kind?

Then she looked around. She had a charming manner of holding her small hands half against her cheeks, half against her neck, and turning slowly from the glass and looking at him with lowered eyelids, and a kind of mischievously proud and yet tenderly suppressed consciousness of victory. "Are you satisfied, Boris?"

What could he answer?

"You come just as if called," then said she. "You shall put the hair-pins in my hair. Katia is so awkward." Then she sat down in a low chair, and handed him the hair-pins. They were wonderful hair-pins, the heads of which were narcissi formed of diamonds, a bridal present from Lensky. He took them with gentle fingers, and the celebrated artist was proud if his young wife praised him for the taste with which he fastened her diamonds in her hair.

.　　　.　　　.　　　.　　　.　　　.

"Natalie!" exclaimed Boris, in a tone of the greatest surprise—a surprise made up of the greatest astonishment and not of joy—"you here?"

It was in his study, and nine o'clock in the morning. At this hour, daily, in crying opposition to his former proverbial unreliability, he had long been sitting at his writing-table. But that Natalie should leave her bedroom before ten o'clock had hitherto been an unheard-of occurrence.

But to-day, just as he was about to go to the piano, to try on that modest representative of an orchestra a completed musical phrase, he discovered her. Quite unobserved, she had mischievously crept in, and now crouched comfortably in a large arm-chair, which formed a very picturesque frame for her silk wrapper, bordered with black fur. She sat on one foot ; one tiny gold-embroidered Caucasian slipper lay before her on the floor, and she smiled tenderly at her husband with her great, proud eyes. But the pride disappeared from her glance at his ejaculation, an ejaculation which expressed so much perplexity, so little joy. She started and, embarrassed, reached out for her slipper with the tip of her foot.

" Do I disturb you ? " she asked, anxiously. " Must I go ? "

Formerly he could not bear to have any one about him when he worked. His face wore a forced, smiling expression, while he assured her :

" Oh, not in the slightest—pray sit down."
Whereupon he pushed his chair up to hers.

" Oh, if you are going to treat me so!"
said she.

" How, then?" asked he.

" Like—like any visitor," she burst out,
and hastened to the door. He brought her
back. Then he saw that her eyes were full
of tears.

" But what is the matter?"

" I am ashamed of my intrusion, that is
all. Adieu—I will not disturb you further!"

With that she wished to free herself from
him. But that was not so easy. He took
her, struggling in his arms like a child, and
carried her back by force to the immense
chair which they had left. " So now, sit
there, and don't spoil my mood, you witch.
Why should I not enjoy your company for
a little? Do you think, then, that I am not
glad to see you? But you do not expect
that I should bend over the table, and spoil
paper, while a charming little woman sits

behind me? The temptation to talk to you is too great."

She shook her head. "You wish to be good to me, but you pain me," murmured she. And she added, flatteringly, "Can you really not work when I am with you?"

"Would you like it if I could?" he asked, and looked at her with a quite new, penetrating expression in his eyes.

He drew his brows together humorously; he was now kneeling before her, and held both her hands in his. "You are not only a charming little woman, Natalie," said he, "but, what very few such beautiful and seductive women are, of a good heart. But still I have noticed one thing in you, namely, that you do not like to be second anywhere. And, do you see, everywhere else you are not only the first, but the only one in the world for me; but here, Natalie, here it must please you that I should forget you for my art!"

"And do you think that I would wish it otherwise?" said she, and there was an earnest, solemn expression in her eyes which he never forgot. " Oh, you blind one, you do not yet know me at all. Do not kneel there like a hero in a romance; in the long run, it looks not only awkward but uncomfortable. Sit down by me—there is room enough in this immense chair for us both. So! and now—now I will confess to you what I have already so long had on my heart. Do you see, you love me, I do not doubt that, how should I ? but—do not be angry with me—sometimes I wish that you loved me differently; I wish to be not only your petted wife, your plaything——"

" My plaything ! " he interrupted her, very reproachfully. " Oh, Natalie ! my sanctuary ! "

" Well, then, as far as I am concerned, your sanctuary. That, looked at in one light, is also only a plaything, even if of the most distinguished kind." She laughed somewhat constrainedly. " It is certainly immoderate," she continued, and hesitated a little, " horribly immoderate, but still it is so—I—I do not want to be only your plaything, but also your friend—do not be horrified at this audacity—yes, your friend, your confidante. I wish to be the first to share your newly arising thoughts. Lately, it has often hurt me that you busy yourself so much with all kinds of trifles only to give me pleasure. I know it is my fault; at first I was afraid of your genius, which soared heavenward, and wished to accustom you to the earth, and chain you close to me. But then—then I was ashamed of my smallness—ah, so ashamed. You shall not stoop down to me; let me try to rise to you. Spread out your mighty wings, and fly up to the stars, but take me with you ! "

He could not speak—only kisses burned on his lips. He pressed them on her wonderful eyes, whose holy light humiliated him. Then, after a while, he murmured, softly : " You are nearer the stars than I, Natalie. Show me the way, show me the way ! "

.   .   .   .   .   .

From then, she daily passed a couple of hours in his study. How happy she felt in the great, airy room, which was almost as empty as a shed. In here she had not ventured with her soft, seductive, decorative arts. All had remained as sober and plain as he had always been accustomed to have his surroundings while at work. High shelves almost breaking under their weight of music, a piano, a couple of stringed instruments, the arm-chair in which he had established her, and two or three cane-bottomed chairs constituted the whole furniture. On the writing-table stood a picture of Natalie, painted in water-colors by a young French artist in Rome. The room could show no other ornament. Still, there in the darkest corner hung a single laurel-wreath. No large one, such as one lays to-day at the feet of great artists, but poor and small, and in the middle of the wreath, in a common wooden frame, drawn with a hard lead-pencil, the face of a woman, with a white cloth on her head, from beneath which fine, curly hair fell over the forehead. Without being beautiful, the face was strangely attractive, and Natalie would have liked to ask the history of the laurel-wreath and the picture. But she did not venture to. She never, by a single question, touched upon Lensky's past.

He only continued to remain in solitude during the hours which he devoted to technical practice. At other times he quietly let her stay. She sat behind him, quite soberly and still, in the large, worn-out patriarchal chair, and did not breathe a word. She never even took a book in her hand, for fear of irritating him by the rattling of turning pages, but busied herself with pretty, noiseless handiwork.

The feeling of her presence was unendingly sweet to him. His whole activity was increased; he worked more intently than formerly. A fulness of music vibrated in his head and heart. And if the inward vibrations became too dreamily sweet, too luxuriant and exuberant, he stopped writ-

ing, sat awhile in silence, and then, without
taking the slightest notice of Natalie, walked
up and down a couple of times, hummed
something to himself, made a sweeping gesture, in conclusion took up the violin—
then——

Natalie raised her head and listened—
how wonderful that sounded ! He had un-
learned the madness, but still in his melodies always sounded the strange Arabian
succession of tones, the devil's music:
Asbeïn !

She became, as she had wished, the confidante of his work. When he had sketched
on paper the plan of a composition, he
played it to her, now on his violin, which
he passionately loved, now on the piano,
which he did not love ; for its short tone,
incapable of development, repulsed him,
but which he respected and made use of
as the most complete of all instruments.
Although he played the piano, not with
virtuosity, but with the helplessness of the
composer, he could still bring out some-

thing of the " warm tone " which made his violin irresistible.

How eagerly she listened to his compositions! How much she rejoiced in them, and how severe she was to him! She would not let him pass over a single musical flaw. That she rejoiced and wept over the beauties in his compositions, that she boldly placed his genius near Beethoven and Schumann, that is to say, near what she ranked highest in the world, that was another thing! For that reason she was so severe. He laughed at her sometimes for her tender delusion. Then she took his head between her hands, and said, triumphantly: " That is all very well; only wait a little while, then the whole world will say that you have been the last musical poet: the others are only bunglers."

In the beginning of March he made a short artist tour through the interior of Russia. Naturally, he could not drag her around with him, for she could not endure

the exhausting fatigues of his quick jour-
neys, especially at that time. But how horrible, how unbearable the parting seemed to
him! He wrote her every day. His writing was ugly and irregular, his orthography
as deficient in French as in Russian; but
what tenderness, what passion and poetry
spoke from every uncultured, stormily written line. No one could better impress his
whole heart in a short, insignificant letter
than he; and what rapture, what wild, almost painful rapture at seeing her again!
She had missed him much less than he
had missed her. He reproached her for it,
complained that the new love which now
began to fill her whole existence left no
place for the old. But then she measured
him with such a tender, and, at the same
time, a so deeply hurt look, that he was
ashamed.

"You must not take it so," he whispered
to her, appeasingly. "It is an old story
that if two hearts hasten forward together
in a race of love, one will naturally outdo

the other, and still will be vexed that it is so. But it is quite natural and in order that I should cling more to you than you to me."

She smiled quite sadly. " We will see who will win the race in the end," murmured she.

.   .   .   .   .   .

Natalie no longer went into society. Her health was much impaired. She passed the entire month of April stretched on her lounge, in loose wrappers. She now reproached herself with having been foolish not to have spared herself before. The time of tormenting fancy approached for the young wife, the time of concealed anxiety for them both. In spite of the consoling assurances of the physician, Lensky was no longer himself, from anxiety and despair. But he did not let her notice it. When he was with her he had always a gay smile on his lips and a droll story for her diversion. He cared for her like a mother.

Then, toward the end of May, came the

most tormenting hour he had ever lived through, until at last—when he already believed that all hope was lost—a little, thin, shrill sound smote his ear. It startled him, his heart beat loudly; still he did not venture to move, but listened, until at last the doctor came out of the adjoining room, and called to him: " All is over."

He misunderstood the words. " She is dead ! " he gasped.

" No, no ! Boris Nikolaivitch ; everything is as well as possible. Come ! "

He felt as would a man buried alive, if one should raise the lid from his coffin.

At the door of the bedroom a fat old woman, with a large cap, came toward him. " A son, a very fine young one ! " said she, triumphantly, while she laid something tiny and rosy, wrapped in white cloth and lace, in his arms.

Tears fell from his eyes, and his hands trembled so that the nurse was horrified and took the child away from him.

He went up to Natalie, who, deathly pale

and exhausted, but with a lovely, indescribable expression on her face, at once of tenderness and of a certain solemn pride, lay
among the high-piled pillows. Quite softly,
with a kind of timidity which his violent
love had hitherto never known, he pressed
her pale hand to his lips.

"Are you content?" she whispered,
dreamily and scarcely audibly. "Are you
content?"

. . . . . .

She recovered rapidly. Her beauty had
lost none of its charm, but had rather won
an earnest—one might almost say consecrated—loveliness.

Her face reflected her happiness. That
also had become a shade deeper, nobler. In
spite of all her pampered habits, she insisted
upon caring for the child herself. He let
her have her way.

The former dressing-room was changed to
a nursery. Sometimes, in the long, transparent twilight of the spring, he entered the
room in which, in winter, he had passed so

many charming hours by candle-light, and
where now everything was so changed. A
cradle stood in the place which formerly
the toilet-table had occupied—ah, what a
cradle—a dream of a cradle! A basket with
a canopy of green silk, hung with a long,
transparent lace veil, a costly nest for a
young bird whose little eyes must be
shielded, by all kinds of tender devices, from
the bright light, which perhaps later would
pain him so!

The air, quite filled with a pleasant, mild,
damp vapor, was permeated by a weak
perfume of iris and warming linen, and,
besides that, with something quite strange,
quite peculiarly sweet, stirring—the breath
of a healthy, fresh, carefully cared-for little
child.

And there, where the cheval-glass had
formerly reflected to him the lovely form
of a proud queen of beauty, now sat in
the same large arm-chair, a tender young
mother, her child on her breast. The lines
of her neck, from which the loose, white

dress had slipped down a little so that the outline of the shoulders was visible, was charming; but what was it to the lovely, attentive expression with which she looked down at the child?

Everything about her expressed tenderness: her look, her smile, the hands with which she held the child to her. It was just these small, white hands which Lensky could not cease to observe. How helpless they had formerly been—and now! She would scarcely let the nurse touch baby. He was never weary of watching how untiringly she touched the tiny, frail body of the infant, and did a thousand services for it which all resembled caresses.

.   .   .   .

"It is all very beautiful, but you have a manner of ignoring me in this little kingdom," said Lensky, jokingly, to the young mother, while he threw a look of humorous vexation at the young despot whom she just laid in the cradle.

She bent her head a little to one side,

and whispered roguishly, while she came up to him and played with the lapel of his coat: "Do you see, Boris, this is my study. Everywhere else you are not only the first but the only one in the world for me; but here you must be content if I sometimes forget you for my calling."

He laughed.

"Do you know that you once said something similar to me; that time when I, for the first time, dared to enter your sanctuary?" she murmured, and repeated petulantly: "Do you know it?"

He kissed both of her hands, one after the other. "Do you then believe that I could ever forget such a thing, my angel?" whispered he. "I am no such spendthrift; oh, no! If you knew how I cherish this dear remembrance! That is pure happiness which we will keep for our old days, when the sun no longer seems to us to shine as brightly, and we must light a poor candle in order to find our path again to a suitable grave."

.   .   .   .   .   .

Natalie still thought of the poor laurel wreath in his study. But she did not venture to ask him a direct question about it.

He himself, of his own accord, at last told her the history of the pitiful relic.

He had never spoken to her of his childhood, but once a great impulse came over him to tell her the whole; to lay bare before her all the pitiableness of his past. What would she then say to it?

It was a clear summer night, out on the terrace of the country house near St. Petersburg, which they had hired for the summer, the terrace which looked out on the small but pretty and shady garden. They sat there, hand in hand; around them the dull, gray light of a day that will not die, sweet perfume of flowers, and in the tree tops the gentle rustling of the kissing leaves. She talked of gay, insignificant things; gave him a droll, laughing description of a visit to one of her friends. At first it amused him; then something, he could not have said what, irritated him against this monstrous principle of gliding so triflingly and mockingly through life without ever glancing into it more deeply.

"What would she say if she knew?" thought he. "Perhaps she would shun me!" A kind of madness overcame him. He felt the wish to risk his happiness in order to convince himself of its durability, to put his petted wife to the test. "How you butterflies, floating over flowers in the sunshine, must be horrified at the miserable worms who creep over the earth!" he began bitterly.

"What are you thinking of?" asked she, astonished.

"Nothing especial, only that I was originally just such a worm, creeping over the earth."

"Ah! that is long past!" she interrupted him hastily. She wished to keep him from long dwelling on an unpleasant thought, but he suspected that his insinuation of his humble antecedents vexed her, and that she felt the need of forgetting his derivation. He looked at her from head to foot, with an angry, wondering glance. Her richly embroidered white dress, the large diamonds in her ears,—how the diamonds sparkled in the dull evening light!

Then he began to speak of his childhood, dryly, with a smile on his lips as if it was a question of something quite indifferent and amusing.

In a large tenement at Moscow, overcrowded with all kinds of human vermin, had he grown up; in the half of a room that was divided by a sail, behind which another poor family hungered. His father he did not remember. His mother sang to the guitar in wine rooms. When he was five years old she had bought him a fiddle for four rubles, and then some one, a dissolute musician, who often came to them, had taught him to scrape on it a little. From that time he accompanied his mother when she sang in the wine rooms,—or even on the streets, as it happened.

She had been pretty; the drawing which

hung in the laurel wreath, and which an
artist in their horrible dwelling-place had
made of her, was like her. Only she had
quite unusually beautiful teeth which one
could not see in the picture. He remembered these teeth very well, because she
laughed so much, especially if there was
little to eat and she made him take it all,
and declared she had spoiled her appetite
at a friend's house with fresh *pirogj*. Once
the thought had occurred to him that she
only said so because there was not enough
for two, and then he could not eat anything more. If there was nothing at all to
eat, either for him or for her, she told him
a story.

Had he loved her? Yes, he believed so
—how could it be otherwise? But the consciousness of what she really had been to
him only came to him when he was no
longer with her. How that happened he
really did not know, but one fine day she
took him in a part of the city which he had
never known until then, in a handsome

residence that seemed so beautiful to him that he only ventured to go around on tip-toes. At the door a fat, yellow man, with long, greasy, black hair, received him, and told his mother it was all right. Then she kissed him a last time, told him she would take him away in an hour, and went.

He was taken in a room with gay furniture, and there greeted by a fat woman with a thick gold chain over the bosom of her violet silk dress, and with rings on all her short, stumpy, wrinkled fingers, and was entertained with tea, cake, and honey. He had never before enjoyed a similar repast. He felt in an elevated frame of mind.

When the fat man—he was a mediocre musician who had married a rich merchant's daughter, who gave him none of her money, however—told him that he should always stay with him, and never go back to his mother, he was glad, and felt the conscious-ness of having taken a step forward in the world.

Did that surprise Natalie? He could

not help it, it was still so. "Strange what roughness men show before a little bit of civilization has taught them to conceal it," he added reflectively.

Did he not feel anxiety later? Natalie wished to know. Yes, for his new life contained nothing of that which he had promised himself. That he should live in the beautiful rooms with the master and mistress and eat with them, as he had thought at first, had been an illusion. Only the two children of the fat daughter of the merchant could tumble around on the sofas, with their fiery-red, woolen, damask covering, and could help themselves from all the dishes.

He lived on charity; they told him that every day. The musician had bought him of his mother for fifty rubles, as Lensky afterward learned, as a speculation, in order to make money out of him as a prodigy. The time which he did not devote to his musical practice he must spend helping the maid in the kitchen.

He slept, with an old sofa pillow under his head, on the floor, in a gloomy little room, without window, only with dirty panes of glass in the door—a room in which the cook put all kinds of rubbish. Dampness ran down the walls, and every evening from all corners crept out a whole regiment of black beetles, and spread themselves over the boards. The food? Well, it was sparing. Sometimes he only received what the family had left on their plates.

Was he not angry at this treatment? No. He found it quite in order at that time. The well-fed, warmly dressed people impressed him, especially the cap of Vauvara Ivanovna—that was the name of his mistress. He felt a respectful shudder pass over him every time he saw this structure of blonde, red flowers, and green ribbon. Except the Kremlin, nothing impressed him so much as this house.

When the whole family, in festival attire, went to church on Sunday, he stood at the

door, quite oppressed by the feeling of
modest wonder, and looked after the well-
dressed, well-fed people. He did his best
to make himself useful and agreeable, and
to please them. Yes, he was just so small
and pitiable, as a half-starved six-year-old
pigmy. And then, in conclusion, one day
he simply could bear it no longer and ran
back to his mother. He found the way.
With that quite animal sense of locality
and traces, which only children of the
lowest classes of men have, he found it.
His mother was at home; she was frightened when she saw him. Had they turned
him out? Yes, she was frightened. In the
first moment she was frightened; then—
here Lensky stammered in his confession—
naturally she was glad; for, what use of
losing words?—naturally she was glad.
How she kissed him and caressed him with
her poor, rough, toil-worn, and still such
gentle, warm hands. He still felt her
hands sometimes on him, in dreams, especially behind his ears and on his neck.

Then she fed him. She spread a red and white flowered cloth over the table in his honor, and after that she gave him a holy picture. Then she said it could not be otherwise; he must go back to Simon Ephremitsch; it was for his own good. When he had become a great artist, then he would come to fetch her in a coach with four horses.

That impressed him. And in order to calm him completely, she promised to visit him very soon.

But she did not come; and when he ran back to her, after about a month, she was no longer in her old abode; he never found her! Soon afterward she sent him two pretty little shirts, delicately embroidered in red and blue. But she herself did not come. Never!

At his first appearance in public—he had performed his piece with the anxious assiduity of a little monkey that fears a blow, he asserted—to his great astonishment, he was applauded. In the midst of the handclapping he suddenly heard a sob. He was convinced that his mother had been at the concert.

At the conclusion they handed him a laurel wreath, the same which now hung in his room; quite a poor woman had brought it, they said. He guessed immediately that the wreath came from his mother; and suddenly, just as a couple of music-lovers had stepped on the stage, in order to see the wonderful little animal near by, he began to stamp his feet and clench his fists, to scream and to sob, until every one crowded around him. His principal threatened him with blows; a very pretty young lady in a blue-silk dress took him on her lap to quiet him; but all was of no use.

He saw his mother once more—in her coffin.

His benefactor told him that she was dead, and that, after all, it was suitable that he should show her the last honors. The coffin stood on a table, surrounded by thin, poorly-burning candles, and she lay within, so small and thin, her hands folded on her breast, in a poor shroud, that they had bought ready made for a few copecks.

In the beginning, Natalie had interrupted him with questions, but now she had long been silent. He looked at her challengingly, at every pitiful, repulsive detail, especially if it brought forward a trace of his own insignificance. It was quite as if he expressly tried to pain her. But when he came to speak of the death of his mother, whose form, in the midst of his glaring, sharp description, he drew so tenderly and vaguely, obliterating everything disturbing, as if he saw her, in remembrance, only through tears, he closed his eyes.

Suddenly he heard near him a suppressed sound of pain, then something like the falling of the over-abundant load of blossoms from a tree among whose spring adornment there yet moves no breath of air.

He started, looked up—there was Natalie

on her knees before him, the beauty, the
queenly, proud one, and had embraced him
with both arms, as if she would shield him
from all the woes of earth, and sobbed as
if she could not console herself for his past
suffering.

"Natalie! my angel, do you really love
me so?"

"One cannot love you enough, or recompense you enough for all that you have
missed," whispered she.

And he had really for one moment suspected that——

He raised her on his knees. They did
not speak another word. Through the garden at their feet the birches rustled in the
mild night breeze, and from the distance
one heard the sad voice of a marsh bird,
who with heavy beating wings flew to the
neighboring pond.

The most beautiful love will always be
that which has been sanctified by a great
compassion. In that mild summer night,
while all around them was fragrance and

veiled light, Natalie's love had received its consecration.

.   .   .   .   .   .

Three, four years passed ; a second little child lay in the pretty, veiled cradle, from which little Nikolai first made his solemn observation of the world—a dear little plump maiden, whom they baptized Mascha, after the grandmother, and whom Boris particularly idolized. There was still nothing to report of Natalie's married life but love, happiness, and beauty. Lensky kept every unpleasant impression far from her, surrounded her with the most touching care, overwhelmed her with the most poetic attentions. Her life at his side unrolled itself like a long, secret, passionate love-poem.

Natalie's family had reconciled themselves to her marriage. Even for the wise and arrogant Sergei Alexandrovitch it had the appearance that he had been mistaken in his discouraging prediction, as happens even to the wisest men, if with their predictions they have only the sober probability in view, without thinking of the possibility of some underlying miracle. After four years of married life Natalie was as happy as a bride.

Still, Lensky's happiness was not as unclouded as that of his wife. A great unpleasantness became ever more significant to him, the quite universal coldness of his artistic relations.

It would be wrong to believe that Natalie, with systematic jealousy, had wished to estrange him from the world of artists. On the contrary, she had complied with his wish to make her acquainted with his colleagues and their families, had herself asked it of him, flatteringly.

The world of artists interested her. There, everything was more animated, more meaning, than the eternal sameness of good society which she knew by heart, quite by heart, she assured him tenderly. She made it her ambition to win his acquaintances for hers. But strangely enough, in spite of all her seductive loveliness, she succeeded only very incompletely.

She had already known the *élite* among the artists. There is nothing further to be said of her relations with these favored of the gods, exceptional existences, than that she always felt honored by intercourse with them, and pleased, and that, when with them she ever vexed herself over the worn-out old commonplace, that one should avoid the acquaintance of famous men in order to prevent disappointment—a commonplace which was probably invented for the consolation of those who, in advance, are excluded from intercourse with celebrities. That Natalie always succeeded in winning the sympathies of these exceptional natures stands for itself.

But when it was a question of that great crowd of artists, of the mixture of sickly vanity, embarrassed affairs, depressing relations, etc., then it was hard to build up a friendship between Lensky's wife and his old colleagues.

Envy of Lensky, envy which had reference largely to his artistic results, and in a

less degree to his marriage and social position, peeped out everywhere from these
people, and had its own results in soon
completely embittering the not very pleasant relations between them and Natalie.

In a truly friendly, touchingly friendly
manner, they only met her in quite mod-
estly circumstanced families — families of
a few true artists who yet could accomplish
nothing with their work but to honestly
and poorly provide for their seven or eight
children. Families of simple people, who
had formerly been good to Lensky in the
difficult beginning of his career, and to
whom he always showed the most faithful
adherence, the most prodigal generosity.
She also felt happy among these plain
people.

What wonder that these people would
all have gone through fire for him! They
would also have all given of their best for
Natalie, whom without envy they wor-
shipped with enthusiasm as a queen. They
rejoiced that Lensky, their pride, their

idol, possessed such a beautiful and distinguished wife—in their èyes the daughter of the emperor would not have been too good for him.

Natalie thanked them for their great attachment, as well as she could ; she reckoned it a special favor to receive these modest people in her home, to invite them with their wives and children, to entertain them with distinction, to stuff all the children's pockets full of bonbons, and give them little parting presents.

But intercourse with these poor devils was in reality only a sentimental game, even as intercourse with the artistic *élite* was nothing but an ideal recreation. Neither the one nor the other sufficed to firmly knit the band between Lensky's wife and his former world, or to keep up his popularity in that world.

. . . . . .

Of all the opposition and difficulty which would arise therefrom for Lensky's future and especially for his yet to be won future as composer, Natalie still suspected nothing. For her, the whole heaven was still blue.

Then the first deep shadow fell on her happiness. Lensky, to whom every long separation from her was unbearable, when he undertook a long tour through central Europe, in spite of her express request, could not resolve to leave her behind with the children, in St. Petersburg. The little children were left under the care of their grandmother.

For the first time, Natalie was no amusing, but a dull and nervous, travelling companion. An unbearable anxiety followed her like a foreboding. All his attempts to console her were in vain.

In Dusseldorf, she received, by telegraph, the news that little Mascha was ill with diphtheria. When she arrived in Petersburg, half dead from anxiety and breathless haste, the child lay in her coffin.

He was almost as desperate as she. He overwhelmed himself with self-reproaches;

—who knows, if they had watched the child better, if they had thought of this or that in caring for it. . . . What torment, to be obliged to say that to one's self! A reproach never passed her lips, she even concealed her tears lest they should sadden him. But from that unhappiness on, something in her formerly so elastic nature, so capable of resistance, was broken forever. The first jubilant time of their marriage was at an end.

.   .   .   .   .   .

Together with the evermore unpleasant friction with his colleagues, and the great pain for his lost child, still another worry announced itself to Lensky—something gnawing, and incessantly tormenting: a daily increasing money embarrassment. Natalie decidedly spent too much, but quite naïvely, with the firm conviction that she could not exist more economically; wherefore it was doubly hard for him to be finally obliged to tell her that he could not raise the money to continue the household on the footing to which she had been accustomed.

It was quite touching to see how frightened she was when he made her the first communication in reference to it—frightened, not at the prospect of having to save, but only at the thoughtlessness by which she had burdened Lensky with cares. She immediately showed herself ready for the most exaggerated reforms. But to live with his wife like a proletary, in St. Petersburg, among her brilliant relations and friends, he could not bring himself to do.

In the autumn of the same year, he moved with his family to ———, a large German capital, where he had accepted the direction of a significant musical undertaking.

But here the conflict between his artistic and family life which had arisen through his alliance with Natalie, came to light with more detestable clearness.

He was in his element, as an artist whose powers have found a wide, noble sway.

The great musical undertaking, at whose head they had placed him, flourished wonderfully under his lead. The fiery earnestness with which he undertook it won him all musical hearts. Also the atmosphere in —————— was sympathetic to him for other reasons. He had a crowd of old connections there, acquaintances of his first virtuoso period, people who surrounded him, distinguished him, with whom he could speak of his art—which always remained sacred and earnest to him, and never, for him, deteriorated to a more or less noble means of earning his living, or to a social pedestal—in quite a different manner than with the elegant dilettantis who had gradually crowded out every other society from his house in St. Petersburg. They gave one artistic festival after the other in his honor, and all this entertained him.

His wife appeared with him a couple of times on such occasions, then she excused herself—she had no pleasure in them. She felt isolated, an insurmountable home-sickness tormented her.

Without confessing it, for the first time since her marriage the position which she occupied with Lensky angered her.

In St. Petersburg she had always remained with him the Princess Assanow, he had ascended to her world; here she must suddenly satisfy herself with his world. She was too vexed, too angrily excited to seek in this world all the true interest, earnestness, and nobility that were to be found therein.

She had intimate intercourse only with an old friend of her youth, a certain Countess Stolnitzky, who went out but little and consequently had time enough for Natalie.

Lensky begged Natalie to open her drawing-room one or two evenings a week, that is to say to his friends. Natalie's drawing-room became a meeting-place for all kinds of artistic leaders, among which the dramatic element formed the principal contingent, and this chiefly because Lensky wished to have an opera performed.

For him, intercourse with dramatic artists had no unpleasantness; he had been accustomed to it from youth. But it became unpleasant to Natalie after she had satisfied that superficial curiosity which every woman living in severely exclusive circles feels concerning these theatrical people.

The only people that were still more unpleasant to Natalie, in her drawing-room, than this crowd of people still smelling of freshly washed-off paint, were the aristocrats who came there to meet the artists. And many of these came—very many, all who coquetted with a little bit of musical interest—yes, and many others. "Very interesting, these *soirées* at Lensky's," they always said, when these were spoken of; "very interesting; they always have very good music there, and then one meets a crowd of amusing people whom one never sees anywhere else. And the wife is really charming—quite *comme il faut.*"

"She is a Russian princess," a foreigner interrupted, who belonged to the diplomatic corps.

The native women turned up their noses repellently. They placed no great confidence in the distinction of Russian princesses who married artists.

Natalie was so ignorant of their rooted prejudices that she greeted the ladies who came to her house with the greatest frankness as her equals. She caused offence by her naïveté, and noticed it. People came to Lensky, not to her—if she would only understand that they wished to be as polite as possible to her, in the somewhat narrow limits of well-bred society—but she must understand it.

She did understand. When she observed that most of the ladies accepted her invitations without returning them, yes, when it happened that the art-loving Princess C. sent Lensky an invitation to a *soirée*, and overlooked his wife, then she understood. It began to tell upon her, to aggravate her.

She fulfilled her duties as hostess with displeasure, did the honors negligently, and did nothing to animate her receptions. My God! people came there to hear music and to rave over her husband,—she was no longer necessary. She became quite foolish and childish.

She was used to the homage that was paid her husband, she would have been fearfully angry if they had not paid him enough; but in Russia, this homage was shown in quite a different, much nobler, intenser form; in Russia he was a great man, before whom every one removed his hat, a sacred being of whom the nation was proud; men and women of the highest rank showed him the same respect.

But in ———, except one or two particularly enthusiastic lovers of music, none of the nobility appeared in his house, with the exception of the ladies. Why did he ask them? He ridiculed them—but yet their flattery pleased him. He had dedicated a composition to more than one of them.

Natalie was almost beside herself with rage. For the first time she felt a certain jealousy. Among others, there was a little dark Polish woman, married to a Swedish diplomat, and separated from him, a Countess Löwenskiold. She purred around him like a kitten.

Formerly he would have noticed the change in Natalie immediately, but for the first time since their marriage he forgot, not only in his study but elsewhere, his wife for his art. He was so happy in his art, so completely occupied with it, that he scarcely noticed the pitiful social pin-pricks which formerly would have caused him vexation enough, and consequently did not consider the importance they had for Natalie.

The study of his opera, for which they had placed at his disposal the best facilities at the command of the ———— Theatre, went steadily forward. The artists liked to work under his direction, and with enthusiasm did their utmost to do justice to his work.   Joy fevered in every vein when he came home from the rehearsals.

.   .   . .

It was toward the end of the carnival. One of Lensky's musical *soirées* had been visited by quite an unusual number of brilliant visitors.   A very large number of ladies of the best society had been there.

They had all appeared in brilliant toilets, with bare shoulders, and diamonds and feathers in their hair.   Natalie was also in evening dress, while the wives of Lensky's colleagues and all the ladies present not belonging to the court circle had come in high-necked dresses.

When the aristocratic ladies, with profuse thanks for the musical treat offered them, had withdrawn before eleven o'clock, because they must, "alas!" still go "into society," into Natalie's social world, but which was closed to her in ———, Natalie remained the only woman in her drawing-room with bare shoulders.

Lensky, who had just accompanied some

tedious Highness politely out of the room,
now returned to the music-room, closed the
door, behind which the noble patroness had
disappeared, and cried gayly: "So, children, now we can be among ourselves, and
enjoy a comfortable evening."

"Among ourselves!" These words
pierced Natalie like a poisoned stiletto.
"Among ourselves!" She bit her lower
lip, angrily.

Meanwhile, pushing back the hair from
his temples with both hands, Lensky asked:
"Would the gentlemen like to play the
Schumann E-flat major quartette with me
before we sit down to supper?" Then he
looked over at Natalie and smiled. She
knew that he proposed this wonderful quartette for her sake, because it was her favorite, but she was already so over-excited
that the touching little attention made no
impression on her. She remained as defiant and bad-tempered as before.

While they played she let her eyes wander gloomily over the already empty hired

cane-bottomed chairs, which stood around
in regular rows. She asked herself bitterly,
what really was the difference between her
"reception evenings" and any other concert?—that the people paid their admission
with compliments instead of money! And
while she made these useless and vexing
observations, the most noble music that
was ever written vibrated around her heart,
like an admonition of how small all these
worldly, outward vanities were in comparison with the lofty, god-like being of true
art! And her obstinate heart had already
begun to understand the sermon and to be
ashamed, when she observed two bold eyes
of a man staring from across the room at
her bare shoulders. The eyes belonged to
a certain Mr. Arnold Spatzig, the most influential musical critic and journalist in
———. Scarcely had he noticed that her
look met his when he left his chair, in
order, crossing the room, to take his place
near Natalie, and continue his insolent scru-
tiny from near by. He was a disagreeable

man, with thick lips, spectacles, and boldly
displayed cynicism.   Natalie, who could
not endure him, had formerly tolerated him
on Lensky's account.   Now she felt so in-
sulted by his manner, that, with the vehement impoliteness of a spoiled woman
whose pride is wounded and who is excluded from her natural sphere, she sprang
up, and turning her back directly to Mr.
Arnold Spatzig, hastened away from him.

And now the quartette was over, and also
the supper which followed, exquisite and
over-abundant as ever, at which Lensky did
the honors with that heartiness, not overlooking the least of his guests, which was
peculiar to him.

It was two o'clock, and the house was
empty; the lights still burned.   Lensky
was busy arranging the music on the piano,
Natalie stood in the middle of the room,
drawn up to her full height, evidently try-
ing to suppress a nervous attack.   She held
her handkerchief to her lips—it was no use.
Suddenly she cried out: "Must I receive

these people? I would rather scrub the floor!" And with that she made a gesture as if she would tear something apart.

"What do you mean?" he asked slowly. He had become deadly pale, and his voice trembled.

She only drew her brows gloomily together and continued to gnaw at her handkerchief.

Then he lost patience. He seized a large Japanese vase, and threw it with such force on the floor that it broke in pieces; then he left the room, slamming the door behind him.

But Natalie looked after him, offended, and broke out in fierce, whimpering sobs.

A few minutes later when she, still weeping and trembling in every limb, leaned against a sofa, in whose cushions she had buried her face, she felt a warm hand on her shoulder. She looked up, Lensky had come up to her. The traces of his difficultly mastered irritation were still on his deathly pale face, but he bent down anx-

iously to her and said gently : " Calm yourself, please, Natalie ; it is no matter. Poor
Natalie ! I should have thought of it
sooner. You shall never again receive any
one—not a person—who does not please
you, only stop crying; that I cannot
bear."

At the first friendly word that he said to
her, her whole ill humor changed to tormenting remorse and shame. "You will
not take what I said to you in earnest,"
said she. "It is not possible that you
should take this madness in earnest. I am
so ashamed—ah, I cannot tell you how
ashamed I am ! I acted unjustifiably, but
I was so tired, so nervous—scold me, be
angry with me, and only then forgive me,
or else your indulgence will oppress me too
heavily," and with that she kissed his hands
and sobbed—sobbed incessantly.

He caressed her like a little child whom
one wishes to soothe, and she continued :
" I will suit myself better to my position, I
will be friendly to every one—as if I could

not make that little sacrifice to your artistic position ! "

Then he interrupted her : " I will accept no sacrifice from you, not the slightest, that I cannot do," said he. " What have you to trouble yourself about my artistic position ? You have nothing at all to do but to love me and be happy—if you still can," he added softly, with a tenderness that for the first time since his marriage had a bitter savor.

But she looked up at him in the midst of her tears, with glorified happiness. " If I still can ? " she whispered, drawing his head down to her—he now sat on the sofa beside her, with his arm around her waist— "if I still can !" His lips met hers, her head sank on his shoulder.

The candles in the chandeliers had burned low down, one of them went out, and in going out threw a couple of sparks down on the pieces of the Japanese vase which Lensky had broken in his anger. He had sent it to Natalie filled with roses,

in Rome, while they were betrothed, therefore she loved it and had brought it with
them to ———.

His eyes rested on the pieces with a
peculiar sad look. "And now lie down
and see that you sleep after your excitement," said he to the young wife. She
followed him like a little child. He mixed
her the sleeping potion of orange essence,
to which she was accustomed, and calmed
her with pleasant patient words. A happy
smile lay on her lips when she at length
fell asleep.

But he did not close his eyes during the
whole night, he did not even lie down ; but
sat in his room at the writing-table. He
wished to work on something, but the
music-paper remained untouched beneath
his pen.

How could she so give way, at the first
little trial which she had ever had ? Why
had she spoken of a sacrifice ?—sacrifice !—
he would take no sacrifice from her.

    .   .   .   .   .   .

Natalie's reception days were given up under pretext of the illness of his young wife. From that time, Lensky saw most of his friends only outside of his house— his " patronesses " he saw no more.

Natalie was ashamed of her small, pitiful discontent, was ashamed of the scene she had made her husband, and still was foolish enough to rejoice over her victory, and to fully profit by it.

She offered all her intellectual, flattering, charming lovableness to recompense for the loss she had caused him, and to quite win him again for herself. She thought of all his preferences in her housekeeping, which, in the beginning, she had somewhat neglected in ——; with half unconscious slyness, she knew how to profit by his small as well as his great qualities ; to attain her aim, knew how to touch his heart as well as to flatter his vanity. In full measure she attained what she strove for. Forgetting all the prudence which his position demanded, he laid just as enthusiastic homage

at her feet as in the very first time of his
marriage. But she was so charming! And
how well her defiant arrogance became her!
that arrogance which would bend to no one
and only with her loved one melted into
passionate submission.

What did the great artist coterie which
his wife had repulsed say to all this? Oh,
who could trouble one's self about all these
people?

Meanwhile, during this happy intoxicated
period he had met with one vexation that
concerned him very nearly. Three weeks
before the appointed date for the production of his " Corsair," the prima donna of
the —— opera, Madame D., an artist of the
first rank, for whom he had quite specially
written the principal feminine *rôle*, declared
that she would not sing it under any consideration. Lensky knew very well that he
had to thank the senseless arrogance of his
wife for the sudden opposition of this irritable leader; it was bitter to him; but without telling Natalie a word of it, he choked

down this unpleasant affair, and submitted
to seeing the part which the artiste had
thoroughly learned and brought to such
splendid . perfection intrusted now to the
weak powers of a talented but awkward
beginner.

. . . . . .

The evening of the representation came.
They were both feverish, he and she; but
she fevered in expectation of a great triumph, he trembled before a defeat.

He knew that his work had three things
against it : a libretto that, for an opera, was
over-finely poetic, and poor in dramatic
effect, the weak representation of the principal *rôle*, and the whole coterie of artists
and bohemians in the audience . excited
against him by the arrogance of his wife.
Perhaps his music would save the situation.
The music was beautiful, that he knew ; he
must build on that.

Natalie made the sign of the cross on his
forehead and hung a consecrated Byzantine
saint's picture, in a strange gold and black

enamel frame, around his neck before he
went into the fire, that is to say, before he
drove to the opera-house to take the baton
in his hand. He smiled at this supersti-
tious action and let it happen.

The greatest heroes like to avail themselves of a little celestial protection before
a battle.

In the opera-house he found everything
in the best condition, courageous, ready for
battle. An hour later he mounted the di-
rector's rostrum.

Once he turned his head to the audience,
and his eyes sought Natalie. There she
sat near the stage in a box in the first row,
which she shared with the Countess Stolnitzky. She wore a black velvet dress, in
her hair sparkled the diamond narcissi
which he had given her as bridegroom;
around her neck was wound a thick string
of pearls which the Empress of Russia had
sent him for her once when he played at
court. In the whole theatre there was no
woman who could compare with her in

proud, beaming, and yet indescribably lovely beauty. She smiled at him constrainedly. What was not hidden in that scarcely perceptible smile! For the last time a kind of happy, proud delirium of love lay hold upon him. He knocked on the desk, raised his arm, and the violins began.

With a kind of magnificent, fiery earnestness, and with that, quite classically severe in the musical roundness and connection of the motives, the overture sounded through the crowded hall. It was rather too long, and as the learned ones among the audience remarked, was better suited for the first movement of a symphony than the introduction of an opera. But what of that! the music was beautiful, wonderfully beautiful, full of sad sweetness and quite demonlike, ravishing power. Here, also, sounded the strange Arabian succession of tones again, which was the characteristic of all his compositions, the devil's tones: Asbeïn.

Natalie did not hear a sound, the buzzing

in her ears, the beating of her heart was too loud.

The last piercing chord resounded through the hall. What was that? An immense burst of applause, unending bravos; the overture had to be repeated.

It was with difficulty that Natalie could keep from sobbing aloud. Again her smile sought his. A beautiful expression of noble, earnest peace was on his features, but his glance did not answer hers, he had forgotten her for his work.

The curtain rose. Natalie scarcely breathed, her hot blood crept slowly through her veins like chilling metal, her ears no longer buzzed, on the contrary her hearing was uncommonly sharp; only she could not take in the music, but listened to all kinds of other things. The rustling of a dress, the rattling of a fan, the whispering of a voice caused her such excitement that it seemed to her, each time, as if she had been shot through the heart by a pistol. The unexpected result of the overture had increased her nervous tension still further.

During the first two acts the opinion remained favorable. After the second act, the Russian ambassador presented himself to Natalie to congratulate her.

While she received his congratulations, still trembling with excitement, she suddenly heard quite loud talking, in a box not far from her.

It was the box of that same Princess C., who was mentioned as particularly musical, and who had invited Lensky to a *soirée* and passed over Natalie. Between her and another art-loving woman sat Mr. Arnold Spatzig. Up to a certain point, he had access to the highest circles of society, that is to say, he was patronized by a couple of ladies who were bored in their "world," and who consequently liked to attract men from some "other world" to them for a short entertainment, not a long engagement, to be amused by them.

"These plebeian men at least take pains

to amuse," the ladies were accustomed to remark, and Arnold Spatzig decidedly took pains to amuse.

Once he raised his opera-glass to his eyes, and stared long and boldly in Natalie's face.

The third act began with an aria by Gualnare, that is to say, with a kind of duet between her and the ocean, which was represented by the orchestra. For a concert piece the number was interesting and original, but peculiarly unsuited to the beginning of the third act of an opera. Only the splendid vocal powers and the poetic comprehension of Madame D., for whom the aria was written, could have saved it; the powers of the beginner who sang the part of Gualnare that evening were not at all equal to her task, her voice, wearied by the exertions of the two preceding acts, sounded almost extinct, her acting was awkward.

Natalie observed the bad impression which this number made on the audience. Anxiously she looked around the theatre :

the people were patient, had too much sympathy for the virtuoso Lensky to inconsiderately insult the composer.

On the stage, still continued the endless ocean duet. Still, in the same monotonous time, Gualnare advanced to the waves and retreated from them, quite as if she were dancing a *pas de deux* with the sea. Then Natalie heard laughing; the laughing sounded from the box of Princess C.

Dr. Spatzig bent over to her, smiling, whispered something to her. She laughed —how heartily she laughed! The opera-glasses of many ladies in the boxes sought the Doctor's critical glance; Spatzig laughed, the Princess laughed, the whole theatre laughed.

The aria was at an end, the gallery applauded. "Ss—ss—ss." What was that cutting, piercing sound which killed the applause?

Natalie became white as chalk; her friend sought her hand; Natalie drew it away; no human sympathy could be of use to her.

From that moment the enthusiasm of the audience rapidly declined. The lack of dramatic action in the libretto became more and more significant. More and more difficultly the poor music dragged along amidst a succession of glaring spectacular effects, which monotonously made place for each other without ever forming an interesting contrast. And the music was so beautiful. There was something so heavily majestic in the rhythm, here and there at once a trifle monotonous and over-laden, but in the accompaniment so wonderfully beautiful in spite of all, and furnished with a richness of melody unattainable by any of the other composers of the time, never approaching the trivial, but always remaining noble.

The audience was weary, and like every wearied audience, mocking; its musical comprehension was worn out. From the middle of the fourth act people began to leave the theatre, and when the curtain fell at the close, not a hand moved.

Countess Stolnitzky accompanied Natalie

silently down the steps. Natalie got into
her carriage and directed it to the stage entrance. She had promised to call for Lensky after the opera. More dead than alive
she sat in the pretty coupé and waited.
The air was sharp, it was a frosty March
night, the stars sparkled as if in cold mockery from the unreachable heavens, quite as
if they were laughing to think that once
more a child of man had tried to storm this
heaven and had so pitiably failed.

A half-hour had passed; at last Natalie
sprang from the carriage and hastened up
the narrow stairs. There she met Lensky.
He was deathly pale, his hat was put on his
head differently from usual, in a kind of
enterprising and challenging manner; his
walk had something negligent, swinging;
there was a vagabond trace in his carriage
that Natalie had never before perceived in
him. He held his cigarette between his
teeth and had the little singer on his arm
who had to-day impersonated Gualnare in
his opera. Many of the singers, as well as

the members of the orchestra, came down the steps behind him, a gaudy, witty, whispering throng. For the first time, Natalie remarked a certain similarity, one might almost say a common family resemblance, between her hero and these other " artists." The men all had the same manner of wearing their hats and swaggering in their walk as he had to-day.

Although these men were more than ever repulsive to her, she greeted them with anxious politeness. " I was afraid you were ill," she said, while she glanced sadly and anxiously at Boris. " I have already waited half an hour for you."

" So ! I am very sorry," replied he, and his voice sounded rougher than formerly. " I sent a messenger to you, he must have missed you. I cannot go home with you this evening, we "—he looked over his shoulder at the following crowd—" are going to have supper together. After a lost battle the commander must care for the strengthening of his troops." He laughed

harshly and forcedly, and touched the hand
of the singer who hung on his arm.

"A lost battle!" said Natalie. "Lost—
but the first two acts were a great success!"

"'Don Juan' did not succeed at the first
representation," remarked some one behind
Lensky. He turned around and looked at
the man with a comical, threatening gesture; then he said, with the expression of a
man with a bad toothache, who yet bursts
out with a witticism: "Who laughs last,
laughs best!"

Natalie still stood, helpless and desperate,
in the middle of the narrow stairs. Her
splendid fur cloak had half slipped down
from her shoulders; her simple, distinguished toilet stood out in strange relief
from the glaring, tumbled, inharmonious,
motley evening adornments of the singers.

"You will take cold, wrap yourself up
better," said Lensky, while he came up to
her and drew the fur up around her neck.

"Will you take me with you to your supper? I would come with the greatest

pleasure ; *je serai gentille avec tout le
monde !*" she whispered, softly and supplicatingly to him.

"What an idea!" said he, repellently.
"No, to-night I sup as a bachelor. You bar
the passage. Drive home quite calmly.
Adieu !"

He pushed her into the carriage, and
went. She put her head out of the window
of the coupé to look after him. She saw
how he got into a fiacre with the singer;
one of the men crawled in after him ; then
she heard some one laughing, harshly,
gipsy-like, was that he? Then came a great
rattling of windows, and creaking and rolling of wheels. Her way and his parted.
Hurrying by a row of ghostly gas-lights,
which all seemed red to her, she rolled away
in a great, cold, black darkness. And ten
minutes later, weary and miserable, she
crept up the steps of her residence. She
knew that something terrible had happened,
something that not only embittered her
present, but would darken the future, that

for her much more had gone wrong than
the result of an opera.

.   .   .   .   .   .

"Who knows, perhaps the thing will pull
through ; even the best operas have sometimes not immediately found approval with
the public," said Lensky, with the awkward,
forced smile that had not left his lips since
the morning after his fiasco. The challenging, gipsy humor with which, in the beginning, he had sought to bluster over his disappointment, had not lasted long. Quiet,
weary, and depressed, he dragged himself
around as if after a severe illness. Natalie
did what she could to be agreeable to him ;
her heart bled with pity, but she did not
venture to approach him.

He avoided her, and if she spoke to him
his answers sounded forced or vexed.

To-day, for the first time since the fatal
evening, he turned to her with a remark in
reference to his work. It was the third
day after the first production of the opera,
and at breakfast. Natalie had just read to

him many criticisms from the newspapers which had arrived. In many, Lensky's magnificent musical gifts were praised.

"Perhaps the thing will pull through," said Lensky, and Natalie replied:

"Naturally, the opera will make a career for itself. You must yourself have forgotten how beautiful your music is, if you can doubt that."

"Is it really beautiful? I really do not know," murmured he. "One is so seldom able to believe it if others shrug their shoulders. To improvise variations on the old theme *mon sonnet est charmant* is a tasteless occupation."

There was a ring at the door-bell; he listened.

"Do you expect anything?" asked Natalie, and then she accidentally looked at the clock. It was already very late, and the hour at which he formerly had been accustomed to sit down to work was long past. She saw very well that he only trifled with time like a man who is too tormented by inward unrest to be able to resolve on an earnest occupation.

"Yes," he replied. "I do not understand why the *Neue Zeit* has not yet arrived."

Natalie lowered her eyes. The *Neue Zeit* was the journal in which Dr. Arnold Spatzig's musical criticism, or rather his musical *feuilletons*, usually appeared.

"That"—Lensky motioned to the pile of other papers—"is all very pretty and pleasant, but it is not decisive. I am anxious to see what Spatzig will say."

"Do you consider Spatzig decisive?" asked Natalie, constrainedly.

"Yes."

"But you told me yourself that his judgment was always one-sided, prejudiced, and superficial; that he was really only a wit and no critic," murmured Natalie.

"I still think so, but nevertheless he has here taken upon himself the monopoly of musical good taste," replied Lensky. "The most intellectual part of the public, that is to say all the subscribers, fancy they can only consider an article of his as true. He has taken out a patent for it, like Marquis, in Paris, for good chocolate. He is witty, which these people like. A criticism is so easily noticed, one always appears intellectual if one cites it, the more malicious it is the better. Until now, Spatzig has spared me, hm—hm—" Boris smiled forcedly. " He even once compared me to Beethoven, but recently he has seemed to avoid me. Have you had anything with him, Natalie ?"

Natalie blushed to the roots of her hair. " I cannot endure him," said she ; " and it is possible that he has noticed it ; in fact, in reference to a certain point, one cannot have patience with a man."

" He surely has not presumed upon you ?" Lensky started up angrily.

" No, no ! He did not have an opportunity," said Natalie, very arrogantly. " Not that ; but he has a way of forcing himself upon one ; of looking at a woman ——"

"That is to say he has bad manners," said Lensky. "Now——"

At this moment there was another ring at the door-bell. Shortly after the servant brought on a salver a whole pile of newspapers in their wrappings, which had just come by post. Lensky opened them hastily; they were all copies of the same paper —of *Fortschritt*, and in every copy there was a twelve-column-long notice marked with a blue or black pencil: "A musical enjoyment by design and intention," and with the motto, for title, "From whence the great discord arises which rings through this world (read opera)."

Hastily, Lensky looked at the signature.

"Arnold Spatzig," murmured he, dully. "I did not know that he also wrote for *Fortschritt*."

"Do not read the thing," said Natalie, who, with feminine quickness, had already glanced over the article. "I beg you; why should you swallow the poison?"

But he shook her roughly from him, bent

over the paper, and read half aloud: "If there were a musical 'Our Father,' the last supplicating request would be: deliver us from all evil, but especially from all virtuoso music. By his opera, Lensky has again given us a significant example of how greatly the reproductive activity of an artist hinders the development of his creative powers. His first smaller compositions really had always a certain melodic freshness. But in this last work, Lensky, like all men poor in invention, has shown himself a follower of that inconsolable musical pessimism which regards *ennui* and a feeling of universal, oppressive discomfort as a *sine qua non* of every distinguished musical work.

" The public, in a sympathetic frame of mind with the loved and distinguished master, in the beginning of the opera strained their good taste so far that they desired the repetition of the extremely tiresome overture, made up of badly connected motives, reminding one of Meyerbeer, Halé-

vy, Gounod. But with the best intentions, the cut-and-dried wonder brought
with them was not proof against the yawn-
ing monotony of the never-ending fourth
act. Only the grotesque side of the unfor-
tunate opera, which ever became more
prominent in the course of the evening,
helped the ill-used public over the dry
emptiness of this musical desert. One
could at least laugh heartily. What a consolation that was for the spectator, but
hardly one for those who took part.

"One cannot understand how such an
artist of the first rank as Mr. —— could
submit to make himself laughable in the
rôle of *Conrad.* . . ."

Lensky became paler and paler; he
reached for a glass of water.

" Do not read any further," begged Natalie. " What does it matter what the liar
writes? your music speaks for itself. This
evening you will see how the public will
applaud you, will receive you, to recompense you for this pitiful insult."

The second representation of " The Corsair " was fixed for that evening.

There was another ring at the door-bell;
the servant brought a letter. Lensky broke
it open hastily, and with a furious gesture
threw it away, struck his fist on the table,
and sprang up.

" What is it?" called Natalie, beside herself.

" Nothing; a trifle; the opera is post-
poned; the tenor has announced himself
ill," said Lensky, cuttingly. " He has no
pleasure in making himself laughable a
second time.   It is over;" passing the palm
of his hand under his chin, with the gesture
by which one understands that some one
has been executed.

Natalie rushed up to him, but he impatiently motioned her away, and hurried by
her to the door. All at once he remained
standing, reached under his collar, tore off
the little gold chain with the saint's picture
which Natalie had hung round his neck before the first representation of " The Cor.

sair," and flung it at her feet. Then he went into his study. She heard how he locked the door behind him.

How benumbed she still stood on the same spot where he had shaken her off from him—he had shaken her off!

How he must suffer to pain her so! Then she bent down to the poor little amulet which he had thrown away. She understood him. She had never been lacking in sentimental-poetic manners, but when it was necessary to sacrifice a humor for him, her love had not sufficed.

Her fault was great, but the punishment was fearful.

THIRD BOOK.

A SHORT time after the fiasco of his opera Lensky resigned his office in ————. His position there had become unbearable to him. He had made no plans for the distant future; for the present he travelled with his family to Paris.

How happy Natalie could have felt here if the still depressed mood of Lensky had not caused her such heavy anxiety. Not that he had further shown himself in the slightest degree disagreeable to her—no, not a single direct reproof crossed his lips; he even, without speaking a word about it, begged her pardon for his momentary roughness by a thousand silent attentions. But what good did that do her? His happiness was gone; he was gloomy and taciturn. Faint-hearted, like all very self-indulgent men, even doubting his formerly revered talent as composer, for the moment he had completely lost his belief in himself.

She did what she could to distract him—all was in vain. And all might have been so pleasant! The Parisian artist world was so large that she quite easily, avoiding all impure elements contained therein, could associate only with those who were lovable, interesting, and sympathetic. Besides, she was now ready for the most exaggerated concessions. If Lensky had wished to write a ballet she would have invited the ballet dancers to breakfast, and been intimate with the première danseuse. The lovely imprudence which, even with her uncommon intellectual gifts, still made the foundation of her petted, undisciplined being, drove her from one exaggeration to another.

He gave a succession of concerts, and all Paris lay at his feet. Natalie sat in one of the first rows in the concert hall and rejoiced over the triumphs of her husband. Occasionally, if the hour for the concert was early, she brought her little son with her

and taught him to be proud of his father.
Little Nikolai looked charming in his Russian costume, with the broad velvet trousers and silk shirt. He always sat there
quite brave and quiet, with the solemn expression of face of a child whom one has
taken to church for the first time; only if
the applause burst out quite too loudly, he
became very excited and stood up on his
chair in order to see his father better.
Then Natalie kissed him, and blushed at
her lack of restraint. And around them the
audience whispered: "That is his child"—
*Tiens! il a de la chance !"—"Ils sont adora-
bles tous les deux !"—"On dit qu'elle est une
princesse !"*

After the concert she went with the little
fellow in the green-room to fetch her husband. The most beautiful women in Paris
crowded around him. He received their
homage quite coolly, and while Natalie,
smiling and polite, did honor to his fame,
he played with his boy, whom he overwhelmed with caresses, without being at

all confused by the presence of strangers. "Admire this if you must admire something!" he burst out once, angry at the intrusive enthusiasm of a very pretty American woman, and with that he raised the child on a table to show him to her. "He is worth the trouble," he growled, and truly such was the case!

One day, about the middle of May, when Natalie, somewhat out of breath, holding her boy with one hand, and a bunch of red roses in the other, came home to lunch, she found Lensky with two strangers in the little hotel drawing-room. One of them was a young man with long hair and short neck, in whom she recognized a famous piano virtuoso; the second, a small, dried-up man, with a yellow, hard, sharp face, she saw for the first time.

At her appearance they both withdrew. Lensky accompanied them out.

"How you have hurried," said he smiling, when he reëntered the room. "You are quite heated!"

"Yes, I hurried very much; I was afraid I would be late to lunch. I know how you hate unpunctuality." And then she sat down on the sofa, and handed her hat and shawl to the nurse, who had come in to get Nikolinka—a nurse by the name of Palagea, in a Russian national costume which created a furore on the boulevard.

"Why did you not take a carriage, little goose?" asked he.

"To economize, Boris Nikolaivitch," replied she, with mischievous earnestness. Then laughing up at him with her great tender eyes, she added: "Besides, the doctor has expressly advised me to take more exercise."

"The doctor?" said he, anxiously. "Do you feel ill? Why did you consult a physician?"

"Yes, why?" murmured she, softly. "Sit down on the sofa by me, so that I can whisper something to you."

"What are you talking about?" said he,

hoarsely, without stirring. "What do you mean? What?"

"You are fabulously uncomprehending to-day," laughed she, and went up to him. "One cannot scream such a thing across the whole room, and as the mountain will not come to Mahomet"—she had now become very red; laying her hand on his shoulder, she whispered: "O Boris; can you still not guess? . . . I am so glad!"

"Natalie!" he burst out. "You do not mean to say" . . . He shook her from him, stamped his foot, and with a furious exclamation left the room.

Ten minutes later, when he entered the little dining-room where they had served lunch, Natalie's maid announced that he must not wait for her mistress, as she was feeling ill. He hurried to her bedroom. She sat on a sofa, her hands in her lap. Her great eyes stared into the distance, she looked like a corpse.

He sat down by her, drew her on his knee, and overwhelmed her with caresses.

"You are right to be angry, quite right.
I was detestable," said he; "but you know
what a bear you have for a husband. It is
only because I love you so dearly that now,
just now, the thing is so inconvenient. Oh,
my little dove, my heart!" He pressed
the palms of her hands to his lips and
stroked her cheeks.

Every vexation melted away in the
warmth of his manner. She suddenly began to sob, but not from grief.

"Do you think, then, that I would not
have been glad?" he said to her tenderly.
"But now, do you see, just now——"

Then he told her the state of affairs.
The man in the Havana brown overcoat
was the famous impressario Morinsky, with
whom Lensky had just made an engagement for a concert tour in the United
States. Morinsky had offered him a small
fortune. "You know how hard it is for me
to part from you," he concluded. "I wished
to take you with me—you and the boy, for
he can put off school for another year. I

thought it was the most favorable moment, and now—it is so stupid, so horribly stupid!"

She had listened very quietly; now she raised her head and said uneasily:

"And now you naturally will have to give up the American project?"

"That is impossible," replied he, turning his face from her, "but I will try—that is, I will put off my departure in any case until the great event is over."

"And then?" She had slipped down from his knee and walked up and down the room uneasily. "And then?" she repeated, while she beat on the floor quite imperiously with the tip of her little foot.

"Then," said he slowly. "Well, then you must either decide to accompany me and leave the children behind, or I must go alone."

"How long will you stay away?" she asked with short breath.

"Eight months, ten months."

"So—ten months!" she spoke slowly.

"And you will part from me—voluntarily, without compelling **necessity**—for ten months?"

Her face had become ashy, the words fell **harsh** and cutting from her dry lips.

"You must not take the thing so desperately," replied Lensky, with an embarrassment which did not escape her. "**Ten** months are soon over."

Something that sounded half like a laugh, half like a cry **of** anguish escaped her **lips.** She stroked the hair back from her temples **with** both hands. Her eyes had suddenly become unnaturally **large,** and were opened uncommonly **wide.** They were no longer the eyes of a usually wise woman.

"Ten months!" she murmured, with extinguished voice, like one who speaks in the midst of an oppressive dream, "ten months —do **you** no longer remember how you used to miss me, if it was only a question of weeks, of days, and not—ten months! But this is no separation, this is a final parting, this is the end of all! Oh, **do not look** at me so!—I am not crazy, I know what I am saying—I know very well! You will come back—certainly you will come back, if no malicious illness snatches you away during your journey; but how will you come back? Like a stranger you will return under your own roof, and a stranger, from that hour, will you remain. You will have acquired other customs, other needs; the tender restrictions of family life will confine you like a forced burden! The good, and magnificent, and beautiful in you will still exist, because it is immortal like everything that is god-like; but it will be grown wild and soiled, and I will no longer be able to force my way through what has towered between me and your heart! And, more than all that, the sweet voice which, until now, has whispered such wonderful songs within you, will be silenced in the confusion of your wandering life; your genius will no longer be able to express itself, it will from then burn in you like a great unrest, and you will feel the treasure which Providence

has implanted in you as an oppressive burden, and will no longer be able to find the
magic word which can lift this treasure!"

He stared gloomily before him.

"Ah, Boris! do not sin against yourself,
because I have sinned against you," Natalie
began once more, with hoarse, broken voice.
"Do not let your wings be broken by this
first disappointment. Your opera was wonderfully beautiful—yes—but it was not the
best that you can give! Give your best, it
will stand so high that the hand of envy
can no longer reach it. Have patience,
sacrifice the virtuoso to the composer in
you, and you will see what a splendid re-
ward you will reap!"

With heavily contracted brows, he listened to this speech, vibrating with desperation. When Natalie had ended, he
remained silent. She believed she had con-
quered. Leaning against him she laid
both arms around his neck, and whispered
to him: "You will stay, Boris—will you
not?—you will stay!"

For a little while he let her stay, then he freed himself from her arms, as one frees one's self from a shackle, and called out: "It cannot be—torment me no longer—I must go!" With that he sprang up to leave the room. At the door he turned round to Natalie, and said: "Are you coming? Lunch will be cold."

"Presently!" said Natalie, "presently!" She shivered, she felt the chill of a great fright in all her members. It was worse than she had believed! Something allured him away. After the first unpleasant surprise at the frustration of his plans had disappeared, he rejoiced at the opportunity of being able to free himself from the chain, and to separate himself from his family for a time. What she had feared for the future had already arrived—the gypsy element in his nature had awakened!

. . . . . .

The agreement between Lensky and the impressario was really completed, the contract was signed, Lensky's departure fixed

for the beginning of October. Meanwhile,
he would pass the summer quietly with his
wife, in the country, in the vicinity of
Paris.

The place which Natalie chose was
about an hour's journey from Paris, and
perhaps fifteen minutes from the railway-
station, a charming old house in the shadi-
est corner of a park, in the midst of which
a large castle stood empty. The castle
was modern; the house, on the contrary, a
carefully reconstructed ruin of the time of
Francis First. The castle was called " Le
Château des Ormes," and the small house
" L'Erémitage." The last owner had re-
stored it, in order that his favorite daughter
might pass her honeymoon there. Since
the daughter had died the Hermitage
stood empty, and to reside in the castle
was painful to the owner. Both were to
let. Lensky left the choice to his wife.
What would she have done with the large
castle ? The Hermitage pleased her better.
The windows were all irregular, one small

and narrow, another very broad, all surrounded by artistically carved and voluted stone framings. The trees grew up high above the roof, and through the whole day sang sweet, dreamy songs, to which a little brook, that ran close by the house, furnished a harmonic accompaniment.

The ground floor was built in accordance with the architecture of the early Renaissance period, with brown beams across the ceilings of the room, and artistic wainscoting on the walls. Gigantic marble mantels, iron chandeliers and sconces, and heavy furniture did what they could to transport the spectator's imagination back to the much sung old times of gay King Francis. At the right and left of the entrance door, set far back in its carved niche, grew lilies, tall and slender; they were in full bloom when the married pair moved in, and their white heads nodded in a friendly manner through the windows of the rooms even with the ground. Sage, lavender, and centifolias bloomed at their feet, tall rose-bushes nodded a fragrant greeting to them from above. The branches of the old trees before the windows were thick enough to partially exclude the sunbeams if they became too intrusive; not thick enough to completely bar the way for them.

In this lonely solitude, Natalie fought a last time for her happiness. She tried to make her whole home as attractive and poetic as possible, so that in Lensky's remembrance something might remain for which he must long. She no longer tormented him with jealous, isolating tenderness, but cared for his distraction and intellectual as well as artistic recreation. She knew how to allure not only the first musicians in Paris, but celebrities of the most different kinds from the capital and surrounding villas, to the Hermitage; earnest men of lofty aims and noble endeavors, together with an animation and susceptibility which did away with the hindering respect which towers between every plain, modest child of man and great people. It always gave Natalie pleasure to see Lensky in the company of these prominent men. He grew in such surroundings.

He was never very talkative; his intellectual capabilities were of a heavy calibre, unsuited for the purposes of small talk. But how he listened, what questions he asked! Then, quite without haste, he would make some remark so peculiarly sharp and far-reaching in reference to some impending political, artistic, or literary question, that, every time, an astonished silence would follow.

One of the guests once remarked: "If Lensky mingles in the conversation, it is as if one fired a cannon between pistol shots."

He was not one-sided in his interests, as other musicians. When one learned to know him more intimately, for every accurate observer it had always the appearance that his musical capabilities formed only a part of his universally abnormally gifted nature.

Quietly and still animatedly passed the days, weeks, and months. Natalie never spoke of the approaching separation.

An inexplicable discomfort tormented Lensky. Natalie had guessed rightly—he had concluded the engagement with Morinsky with quite precipitate haste, not only in order thereby to win the opportunity of acquiring with one stroke a large sum of money which would put an end to his pecuniary difficulties, but because in intercourse with the old friends of his bachelor days in ———— he had first significantly realized how much he had had to restrain himself to live morally and uprightly at the side of his wife; and because his gypsy nature, bound for years, now demanded its rights.

Still it vexed him that Natalie remained so calm in the face of the approaching parting. Now, when the farewell drew near, his heart failed him. Did she, then, no longer love him?

The thought was unbearable to him, prevented him from working. He wrote everything wrong on the note paper.

The lilies were dead, the days became short, and the first leaves fell in the grass, but the foliage was still thick, only here and there one saw a yellow spot in a bluish green tree, and the rustling had no longer the old soft sound.

"The trees have lost their voice, they have become hoarse, the old melting sound is gone!" said Natalie. The roses, in truth bloomed more beautifully than in summer; still one saw, significantly, the approach of autumn, and Lensky had the repugnant feeling that near by something lay dying.

His work did not please him. Three times already he had heard Natalie pass by his door; each time he had thought, now she will come in; he had already stretched his arms out to her, but she did not come. He threw away his pen and sprang up to look for her.

It was a late September afternoon. It

had rained for three days, and the air was cool.

Natalie sat in the brown-wainscoted ground-floor sitting-room, in one of the gigantic, high-backed arm-chairs near the chimney, in which flickered a gay wood fire. The windows were open. The noise from without of the rain drops softly gliding down between the leaves, the blustering of the high swollen brook, mingled with the crackling and popping of the burning wood.

In the middle of the room, on a large table with a dark-red cover, stood a copper bowl filled with champagne-colored *Gloire de Dijon* roses. From without came the melancholy odor of autumnal decay and mingled with the sweet breath of the flowers.

The veil of twilight sank down from the mighty rafters of the ceiling. The corners of the large, somewhat low room were already, as it were, rounded off by brown shadows. Freakish, pale reflections slid over the dark wainscoting, and over the brass and copper dishes which adorned it.

Little Kolia crouched on a stool before his mother, and with both tiny elbows rested on her lap, gazed earnestly and attentively up at her.

One could think of nothing more charming than this mother and this child. Involuntarily Lensky's heart beat high in his breast. "How beautiful my home is, how happy I am here. Why am I really going away?" he asked himself.

"Ah!" cried Natalie when he entered, pleased and at the same time surprised, for his appearance at this hour was something quite unusual. "Do you wish anything?"

He shook his brown, defiant head silently and sat down near the chimney opposite her. The little boy had sprung up, embarrassed, and now leaned against his mother, with his little arm round her neck.

"You have been telling him fairy tales," began Lensky.

"Oh, no! I told him of the ocean, and how one lives and is housed on the wide boundless water—of the ocean and of America. Before it was too dark we were busy with something much more important," said Natalie, and she pointed to a low child's table which was covered with writing materials and lined paper. "Show papa what we have finished, Nikolinka."

The little boy became very red and drew his brows together. "But, mamma," said he, excitedly stamping his foot, "why do you tell that? It is a surprise."

His mother stroked the offended child's cheek soothingly. "We will not give papa your letter to read, only show it to him, so that he can be pleased with it. Bring it, Nikolinka."

Resistingly the little fellow freed himself from his mother, then he brought the document, which was concealed behind a vase, and carried it, with importance as well as embarrassment, to his father. On the already extensively sealed envelope, between three lines, stood the unformed, but neatly and industriously written letters:

À

MONSIEUR BORIS LENSKY,

EN

AMÉRIQUE.

" The letter is to be sent to you when you are over there," explained Natalie.

" How nicely the wight writes for his five years," said Lensky touched, looking at the envelope. " You guided his hand, Na-tascha ? "

" Oh, no ! " declared Natalie.

" But you prompted him ? "

" Certainly not ; he thought it out all by himself ; did you not, Nikolinka ? " said Na-talie.

The little one nodded earnestly ; he was quite crimson with pride and embarrass-ment. His father took him between his knees, called him " Umnitza," which in Russian means paragon of wisdom, kissed and caressed him, then rang the bell for

Palagea, and told him he must go now and wash his hands, and have his curls brushed smooth, and then he should take dinner with his parents, because he had been so clever.

When the child had tripped out at the nurse's hand, Lensky threw himself down on the stool at his wife's feet. It had now become quite dark. The heavy, regular-falling rain still rustled in the foliage without, in a dreamy, melancholy cadence.

"Listen; how sweet, how sad!" said Natalie, turning her head to the window, through which the landscape, behind its double veil of rain and twilight, looked to one like a greenish-gray chaos only, without any distinct outlines.

"The D-flat major prelude of Chopin," said Lensky.

She shook her head. "No, I did not think of that," whispered she. "But see! Sometimes it seems to me that the ghost of the poor young wife who died here creeps around the Hermitage, and sighs for the happiness which she might not finish enjoying. She died after the first year, while I, Boris—I was happy six years. It is too much for one human life. Sometimes—it is a sin; I know it—and still, sometimes I quite wished I might die, but I dare not; Kolia still needs me."

.   .   .   .   .   .

Soon after this she brought a little girl into the world, who was baptized Marie, after the grandmother and the little dead sister.

A few weeks passed, she convalesced rapidly. The day of farewell came, on which every one hastened, with everything overhurried, incessantly imagined there was too much to do in preparing for the journey, and finally had nothing more to do. The day on which all the usual occupations were sacrificed in honor of the pain of parting, when one aimlessly trifled away the hours, tormented by nervous unrest, which finally expressed itself in the dullest *ennui*.

.   .   .   .   .   .

They sat together; now here, now there, and did not know what to do. Lensky was to take the six o'clock train to Paris; from there, the same evening, he would travel with Morinsky's troupe to Boulogne, for they would take ship in Liverpool for America.

The dinner-hour was changed from seven to four, lunch and breakfast were combined at ten o'clock. These irregular hours took away one's appetite, accustomed to regular hours, and increased the general discomfort.

In order to kill the last half-hour before dinner they took a walk through the immense, solitary park. Kolia went with them.

It was a beautiful October day, with a blue heaven over which only filmy white clouds spread themselves, and from which the sun looked down so sadly and mildly as only the October sun looks down on the dying beauty of the year. Masses of foliage still hung on the trees, but it was already withered—it no longer lived. And in the midst of the windless peace, one heard, again and again, the gentle sighing of a dead leaf that fell on the turf.

Both the parents were silent, only the little boy asked, from time to time, tender, important questions of his father, whom he loved very much, although he felt a kind of shyness of him. At first Lensky led the child by the hand, then he took him in his arms, in order to have the pleasure of holding the supple little body quite closely to him and feel the soft, warm little arms round his neck.

They hurried back to the house so as not to delay dinner, and naturally arrived much too early.

"Play me something for a farewell," begged Natalie.

"One of the Chopin nocturnes which I transposed for your sake?" asked he.

"No, just what you have in your heart," replied Natalie.

He took up his violin. It was the same violin which he had tried·in the Palazzo Morsini, the Amati which Natalie had given him when they were betrothed. He was very excited, and became paler with every stroke.

The whole desperation of a great nature which feels an unavoidable degradation approaching, spoke from his improvisation, and in the midst of the passionate and painful madness rose melodies so pure, so beautifully holy, like the resting in heart-felt prayer of a nature all in uproar.

When he had finished and wished to put the violin back in the case in which he should take it with him to America, Natalie took it from his hand.

"What do you wish with it?" he asked.

She kissed the violin and then handed it to him. "Here you have it," said she, very softly. "It will never sing so again until you return."

At last the servant announced that dinner was served. They sat down to the executioner meal, the executioner meal for which all his little favorite dishes had been prepared, at which everything was so abundant and so good, only the appetite was lacking.

It was still light when they went to dinner. The light slowly died in the course
of the meal. The words fell seldomer
and more seldom from Lensky's lips; there
was a leaden silence; the brook sobbed
without.

Lensky held his wine-glass toward Natalie. "To a happy meeting!" said he; "to
a happy meeting!" She repeated, dully:
"I will await you here next year when the
roses bloom." He pressed her hand; he
could not contain himself during the whole
meal, but got up before the dessert and
began to walk up and down restlessly.

"You have still time," Natalie assured
him; "the coffee will come immediately."

"Thanks; is baby asleep? I would like
to give her a kiss before I go."

They brought little Maschenka. He kissed
and blessed the tiny, rosy child, bundled up
in lace and muslin. He has kissed Kolia,
loudly crying from excitement, and commissioned him to be brave and not to grieve his
mother.

Now he goes up to his wife. They have brought the lamps; he wishes to see her distinctly before he goes. She tries to smile; she raises her arms to stretch them out to him—the arms sink.

" My heart, be reasonable," says he, and draws her to him. A fearful groan comes from her lips; she presses her mouth against his shoulder so as not to scream aloud; her form shook.

He held her to him so tightly that she could scarcely breathe. For one moment he is all hers—it is the last in her life! She knows it ! The happiness of her love rallies once more in a feeling of awful, delirious happiness, and dies in a kiss!

Now he has gone ! She accompanied him to the house-door. There she now stands and gazes along the street, through the twilight, where he has disappeared between the trees. It did not seem to her that she had parted from a dear man who was about to make a journey. No; as if they had carried a corpse out of the house. It is all over—all! Whatever further comes is only more dry bitterness and inconsolable torment of the heart. She sees his footprints in the half darkness. Why had she not accompanied him to the railway? she asks herself, why—why? From stupid anxiety, from pride of giving the few loafers at the station the sight of her despair had she renounced the pleasure of enjoying his presence until the last moment? She steps outdoors, hurries her steps, wishes to hurry after him, to see him once more, only one moment—then the loud voice of the railroad bell breaks the universal silence—a shrill whistle—it is over! She falls down, buries her face in the cool autumn grass at the edge of the garden path, and sobs as one sobs over a fresh grave.

.　　.　　.　　.　　.　　.

About three hours later, Lensky, with his colleagues and Morinsky, sat penned up in a coupé of the first class. The train was over-full, there were eight of them in the small compartment.

In one corner slept Morinsky, his fur collar drawn up over his ears, his head covered with a fez, whose blue tassel waved to and fro over his left ear, which lent his sharp yellow face a diabolical expression.

Opposite him sat an old woman with a copper colored skin, and held a basket of lunch on her knees. At first she had uninterruptedly chewed and smacked her lips, now she snored. She was the mother of a famous staccato singer, who, large and blond, with her head and shoulders prudently wrapped in a red fascinator, embroidered with gold, and painted, and smelling of cosmetics, coquetted with the 'cellist, a very effeminate young man who looked like an actor. They had spread a shawl over their knees, and the diva laid the cards for him, which gave occasion for the most entertaining allusions.

The accompanist of the troupe, a pedantic young pianist, afflicted with a chronic hoarseness, which alone prevented him from becoming a tenor of the first rank, formed the public to the beautiful duet, while he laughed loudly at every particularly poor witticism.

The 'cellist and the diva were very familiar with each other, and both constantly made use of expressions of the commonest kind.

The laughter of the diva became ever shriller, while that of the 'cellist sounded ever deeper from his boots.

Opposite Lensky, the short-armed, fat piano virtuoso of the troupe, a very solid father of a family, who tried to sleep, and from time to time looked round angrily at the disturbers of his rest ; and near Lensky, wrapped in furs to the tip of her nose, sat a new prima donna, Signora Zingarelli, of whom Morinsky promised himself the highest success, a beautiful, red-haired Belgian, with long, narrow sphinx eyes. She had tried to enter into conversation with Lensky, but he had turned from her, monosyllabic and coarse.

The train sighed and groaned. Fiery
clouds flew by the window in the black
night. The close atmosphere in the coupé,
the odor of paint, musk, fat meat, hot fur
and coal, maddened Lensky; he wished to
open one of the windows—the singers pro-
tested, Morinsky awoke, settled the dis-
pute :—the window remained closed.

A terrible longing for his love, for his
beautiful, poetic home, came over Lensky.
He thought of his last night journey, with
wife and child, quite alone in a coupé. He
saw the charming serpentine lines which
the slender, supple figure of his young wife
described on the cushions. She slept. Her
little head rested on a red silk cushion
which she took about with her on all her
travels. How tender and delicate her profile stood out from that colored ground!
She coughed in her sleep; he stood up to
draw the fur mantle which covered her
closer up around her shoulders. Drunk
with sleep, she opened her eyes and with
half unconscious tenderness rubbed her

smooth, cool cheeks against her hand. The sweet fragrance of violets which exhaled from her person smote his face. Then— a jolt!—He started up—he must have slept. In any case he had dreamed. His travelling companions all slept now; their heads on their breasts, only the pretty red-haired head of the Zingarelli lay on Lensky's shoulder. She opened her long, narrow eyes, smiled at him—a shrill whistle— the train stopped.

"Amiens!" cried the conductor. "Amiens!" All got out.

While his colleagues plundered the restaurant, Lensky, smoking a cigarette, wandered around the platform alone. The others had all taken their places again, when Morinsky, who had gotten out to look for him, and saw him wandering to another coupé, called after him: "Here, Monsieur Lensky, here!"

But Lensky only stamped his foot impatiently: "Leave me in peace, I am not obliged to make the whole journey in the same cage with your menagerie!" he said.

.　　　.　　　.　　　.　　　.

Six weeks later not a trace of his home-sickness remained. At the artist banquet, which usually followed the concerts, symposiums which began with bad witticisms and ended with an orgy, he was the most unrestrained, the wantonest of all.

He was like one who, suddenly relieved from the pressure of iron fetters, at first, unaccustomed to every free movement, can scarcely move his limbs, but afterward cannot weary of stretching them, and moving them in unlimited freedom.

He broke every bond, indulged every humor. He no longer thought of Natalie and the children, he did not wish to think of them. Remembrance was ashamed to follow him on the way he now went.

It was hard for him to write to his wife, but it was still harder for him to read her letters. And yet she wrote so charmingly, so lovingly! She did not say much of herself, but so much the more of the children, especially of Kolia. With what shining eyes he listened, when she read the reports of the triumphs of his father to him, she wrote, and how he seized every newspaper that he saw, and then asked her: "Is there anything in it about papa?" and how, with his little playmates—she passed the winter with her mother, in Cannes—he boasted importantly of the homage which fell share to his father, and how she did not have the heart to reprove him for it. How he drew ships incessantly, and how she made use of the interest which he took in his father's journey to give him his first lessons in geography, and many other such tender trifles.

These letters vexed him; when he had read them, he despised himself and his surroundings, and for two, three days, remained melancholy and unsociable.

At last he no longer read them, at most only glanced over them, convinced himself hastily that "all was as usual," and then folded them up and laid them aside.

Then came the time when he told himself it was foolish to have such scruples. He was what he always had been, an exceptional man, a Titanic nature. He could not be judged like the others, he could not have exercised his compelling charm over the masses without the fiery violence of his temperament. His success was wonderful. Since they had celebrated the reception of Jenny Lind with discharge of cannon in New York or Boston—history differs as to which, is always careless in relation to prima donnas—no artist had received more homage than Boris Lensky. The women especially seemed as if bewitched by him.

He did not take the situation sentimentally, but rather cynically; still he accustomed himself to the horrible noise of the public, which followed his performances, to the cries of the crowd which accompanied him without, when he left the concert hall, to the illuminated streets in which every window was filled with gazers when he drove home.

When the excitement was once over, a kind of shame overpowered him. What signified these virtuoso triumphs? People always applauded the stupidest piece the loudest. He attained no such effect with a sonata of Beethoven, or Schumann, as with a mad tarentella which he had composed long ago for his wonderful fingers, and of which he was now ashamed.

In Boston, he omitted this tarentella, which had become a nightmare to him, from the programme.

The people remained lukewarm, and so much already did his over-excited nerves desire the shrill storm of applause, that he voluntarily added the trivial and wearying piece of artifice—he, who had formerly so despised his virtuoso triumphs!

.   .   .   .   .   .

The lilies stand straight and slender, with golden hearts in their deep, white calices, right and left of the door of the little Her-mitage, into which Natalie has again moved when the first roses bloom.

It is July.　Lensky has fixed his return for the fifteenth.　"Afternoon, with the first train that I can catch; but do not worry if I should be late," said his letter.

Not at the station, no, only to the hedge which incloses the park, will Natalie go to meet him.

Kolia quivers with impatience.　Natalie counts the hours, draws out her watch—it has stopped.　She hurries in the dining-room to consult the clock on the mantel, and discovers Kolia, who, kneeling on a chair, moves the hands.

"What are you doing?" says she, laughing.

The boy sighs impatiently.　"I am fixing the clock, mamma.　I am sure it must be sick, it goes too slowly to-day."

How she kisses him for it!　How pleased she will be to tell Boris of it!

"Hark!"

A shrill sound of a bell, a penetrating whistle; the train has come.

She fetches her little daughter, who has

had a charming little white dress put on her, in honor of her father's arrival.

With the little one on her arm, and Kolia at her hand, she steps out under the lindens, which are in full bloom, and throw a sunlit shadowy carpet over the path. Oh, how her poor heart beats! She kisses the tiny hands of her little daughter from excitement, looks scrutinizingly at the little child. Will he think her pretty?

She stands at the hedge of the park, looks out on the street, gazes, waits, sees the people return from the railroad. Now he must come! but no, the white, dusty street is empty; a scornfully whispering breeze blows away the footprints of the last passer-by, a couple of white linden-blossoms fall from the tree-tops—he has not come!

And with slow steps, as one wearily drags himself along after a great disappointment, she turns toward the house. Kolia gives a deep sigh. "I don't understand it, mamma," says he.

" Papa will come with the next train ; he has missed this one," his mother consoles him.

For a while he trips silently beside her, then suddenly raising his head and looking at her with his earnest, thoughtful child's eyes, he says :

" We would not have missed the train, would we, mamma ? "

And once more the bell sounds in the solemn quiet, and Natalie's heart beats loudly—and he comes not.

Ever sadder, she wanders through the empty rooms, into which the sunlight presses through a shady, cool, perfumed curtain of foliage.

" How can one stay an hour longer than one must in the sultry, dusty, sunny, wearying Paris ? " she asks herself.

.   .   .   .   .   .

Meanwhile Lensky sits with his colleagues in the *Trois Frères* at a breakfast which began at one o'clock, and now at five o'clock has not yet ended. A breakfast at which all laugh and make jokes—only he broods silently.

He is satiated with this rope-dancer's existence—heartily satiated—he longs for his home, for his dear, incomparable wife, but he delays the moment of meeting as long as he can. A kind of shame contracts his throat at the thought of meeting her eyes. He knows she will ask him no questions, but still——

.   .   .   .   .   .

Once more the railway bell has in vain startled Natalie and her little son. Evening has come. The excellent little dinner which was prepared in honor of the return has been served and taken away quite untouched. Kolia incessantly pulls his mother's sleeve and asks ever more importunately: "Why does not father come? Why does he not come?"

Maschenka has long been divested of her white muslin finery, and lies in her cradle. Kolia obstinately refuses to go to bed until his father has returned. Weary and tearful

he wanders from one corner of the drawing-
room to the other and will not play.

Now, with little head on his arm, he has
fallen asleep over his picture books at a low
child's table.

The roses which Natalie arranged so carefully in the vases wither. The white dra-
peries of her dress are limp and tumbled.

Once again the bell rings. It is the last
train to-day. She does not wake Kolia.
Why should he uselessly vex himself this
time also?

Softly she steps on the porch. The
moon stands in the heavens; the trees are
black. A gray, transparent mist arises
from the earth which obliterates all con-
tours. The flowers smell unusually sweet,
and, in luxuriant melancholy, confess so
much to the pale, cold moon that they have
shamefacedly been silent about to the sun.

Why does the little brook sob so loudly?
Can it not be silent a moment? Natalie's
whole being is now only a strained, longing
listening. Why does her heart beat so

loudly? Why does her strong imagination charm up things in the stillness which do not exist? Or—no—no; she hears a sigh, a step, slow, slow! Who can that be? No man walks so slowly who after long, oh, how long absence, returns to wife and child! It is a messenger of misfortune, who delays to announce some ill news to her.

Then, from out the shadow, in the foggy moonlight, comes a broad-shouldered form.

"Boris!" calls Natalie, half to herself. She cannot go to meet him—she cannot. Trembling in her whole body, she stands there, in the carved Gothic portal, against the bright golden background of the lighted hall; stands there in her white dress, between the tall, pale lilies, like an angel before the door of a church, into which a wicked sinner would like to slip.

"Is it you, at last?" she breathes out.

"Yes; I am somewhat late. You know, with one's colleagues, one must offend no one; it is always so."

How rough his voice sounds! How fleetingly, how hastily he kisses her. Is she dreaming?

"How are you; how are the children?" He steps in the hall, blinking uneasily in the light.

Is this really the man to whose coming she has so foolishly, so breathlessly looked forward? This irritable, heavy man with the tumbled clothes, the badly arranged hair, the fearfully altered face, with a new expression of God knows what! Her feet refuse her their service; she catches hold of a support, and sinks down in a chair.

"How pale you are, Natalie!" says he. "Are you ill?"

"No—no—only—I have waited for you since five o'clock. I—I thought you would never find the way back to us."

For an instant he hesitates; then he sinks at her feet, embraces her knees with both arms. He, who at parting had not shed a tear, now, at their meeting, sobs like a desperate one. What pretext, what falsehood can he utter? As if his colleagues could have withheld him if he had only really wished to come home!

"O Natalie! Natalie! Pardon me. We all fear to return to Heaven when we have accustomed ourselves to Earth. Natalie! be good to me; never let me leave you again."

He had plunged a dagger in her heart, but her whole tenderness is awakened.

She bends over him, strokes his rough hair with her tender, white hand. "My poor genius!" she whispers gently. "My poor, dear genius!"

"Papa!" calls a silvery voice, joyfully. "Pa—pa!" he repeats, hesitatingly, frightened. Kolia has run up.

If he lives to be a hundred years old he will never forget how he saw his father sobbing at his mother's feet after the first long separation.

Then he did not understand, but later he understood—understood only too well.

How sad life is: how sad!

.   .   .   .   ..   :.   .

It was the morning after his arrival. Lensky stood at the window of his room, and looked down in the quiet garden. The little brook which tumbled down the hill at the side of the Hermitage with exaggerated violence, quite like a little waterfall, in front of the house from whence Lensky looked down on it, plashed quite calmly, earnestly, and dreamily along its here scarcely susceptibly descending bed, and bore away on its dark waves only as much of the sunshine as could reach it between the lindens. A cool breeze rose from the water, all around was dark green, dewy and luxuriant—luxuriant without the slightest indication of decay, without the least trace of approaching withering.

And what an abundance of roses stood out in gay, blooming colors against the sober, dark-green background! Great Maréchal Niel roses, with heavy, earthward-bent heads, dark-red Jacqueminot, fiery Baroness Rothschild, delicate pink, capriciously crumpled La France. The Gloire de Dijon roses climbed quite in the window of his room in their race with the quite small, pert little running roses.

Light steps crunched the gravel, large and small steps. Natalie stepped out from the shady lindens in front of the house. She held her little daughter in her arms. Kolia walked near her, and with the important earnestness of six years carried a basketful of strawberries, which he had evidently just helped his mother pick. One could think of nothing more charming than the young woman in her white morning-dress, with its lilac ribbons, and the tiny, rosy being in her arms. The little thing was bareheaded, and her little arms and feet were also bare. She quivered and danced with animation. There she discovered a butterfly, cried out gayly, and clapped her little hands.

"Oh, are you ready so soon?" called Natalie, when she saw her husband at the window. "Come to breakfast; I have had the table laid in the garden."

He hurried down. The breakfast-table
stood in a shady spot, over which the blooming lindens reached their branches.

Oh, what a table! How very pretty the
Rouen service made it! a service whose
old-fashioned gayness combined harmoni-
ously the most incongruous colors, set out
on the dazzling white damask table-cloth.
How inviting and appetizing everything
was! These curiously shaped dishes, with
their fragrant burden of still warm golden
cakes and rolls of pale yellow butter between glittering pieces of ice, and ham covered with transparent aspic! Around the
greenish twilight, fragrant, cool, only here
and there the reddish glimmer of a sunbeam curiously wandered into the shadow,
and now held captive by the lindens.

When she saw her father coming, little
Mascha became quite unruly, almost danced
out of her mother's arms, and, without resisting, let herself be taken, hugged, and
kissed by him. While he held her in his
arms, Kolia seized her little bare legs,

and pressed his mouth to her tiny pink feet.

"She is charming, a beauty! Is that really my daughter, can something so wonderfully pretty have such an ugly man for father?" he said from time to time, laughingly, tenderly, while he kissed her bare shoulders, and especially the dimple in her neck, again and again.

"She looks very like you, your pretty daughter," jested Natalie. "More than the boy! It vexes him if I say that, and I also would prefer it to be the other way."

Lensky laughed somewhat constrainedly. The nurse came up to get baby.

"Just a moment," said Lensky, swinging the little thing high in the air, to its great delight, "so—and one more kiss on the eyes, the neck, on these dear, sweet little hands, so——"

The nurse already had the little thing in her arms, when the sweet little rogue looked round at her father.

Meanwhile, Natalie busied herself with

the samovar, which stood on a small stand
near the breakfast table. No servant was
near, Kolia helped mamma serve tea, and
waited with a sober expression until his
mother had confided the cup for his father
to him. Carefully, as if he held the Holy
Grail in his hands, he carried it over to
Lensky. Natalie sat down opposite her
husband, and buttered him a piece of bread.

He looked at her with a peculiarly sad,
touched look. "You are all much too good
to me," he murmured ; then he added, tenderly : " Either I had really forgotten during my absence how beautiful you are, or
you have really gained in charm."

How awkwardly that came out! how
stumblingly! He had wished to say something loving to her, but he had not succeeded well. He felt it himself. A petulant smile shone in her sad eyes at his well,
or much rather, badly put little speech.
Some reply trembled on her lips, then she
suddenly closed her lovely mouth, as if she
feared her husband would take what she

wished to say somewhat ill, and busied herself in fastening a napkin round **Kolia's** neck.

After a while Lensky began anew : " How charming my home is. Ah, Natalie, how have I renounced it all for so long! How could I exist so long without you !"

" If you only are really pleased over your return we will make no further remarks about your absence," said Natalie very lovingly, and then hesitated with embarrassment and blushed to the roots of her hair.

Breakfast took its course. Here and there, by turns, Natalie and Lensky made a remark, but the conversation did not become fluent. A strange irritation vibrated in every nerve of the virtuoso. Formerly there had been no end of talking between them, and now— What was she thinking of, to speak about the weather as if he were any guest to whom one feels obliged to be polite, and to whom one does not know what to say, because no common interest unites him with us?

He remembered the words which she had spoken in the Hotel Windsor at that time before the conclusion of his contract with Morinsky: "As a stranger you will return to us, and a stranger you will remain among us from that time."

Was she right? Foolishness! She had only become a little too distinguished among the wearisome crowd with whom she had passed the winter. The forced mood which reigned between them was her fault, not his.

"You are so stiff and formal, Natalie," he remarked at last, vexedly, quite irrelevantly. "You have again accustomed yourself to such fearfully aristocratic manners."

"How can you say anything so foolish?" she answered him, laughing constrainedly.

"Oh, it is not laughable to me," he growled, and suddenly, without any reason, only to air his inward uneasiness, he burst out: "It is painful to me, I cannot endure it—cannot bear it." He pushed his cup away with an involuntary motion.

"But, Boris!" Natalie admonished him. "My poor, unaccountable, dear genius!" She looked at him so roguishly therewith that his anger was scattered to the four winds.

He stretched out both his hands to her across the table; she took them. He bent somewhat forward, wished to draw her hands to his lips, when a light step was heard on the gravel. Natalie blushed, and with a quick, almost frightened movement, drew them away from him. He scowled angrily. Before whom was she embarrassed then?

A young woman in a very elegant *negligé* costume, profusely trimmed with Valenciennes lace, without hat, and a yellow parasol in her hand, stepped up to the breakfast table. She resembled Natalie, although she was smaller, stouter, and the features of her pretty face were coarser. Lensky recognized in her his wife's sister, Princess Jeliagin, a person whom he detested from the bottom of his heart, even if he had until

now only known her slightly, before his
marriage with Natalie. Kind friends had
told him that she had described his alliance
with her sister as *une chose absurde.* Wife of
a rich, quite incompetent diplomat, she had
during her ten years' life in foreign countries made all the most absurd aristocratic
prejudices her own, and was always ad-
dressed as " Princess," although her husband had no title. With all these Western-
Europe grimaces she combined something
of her Russian, half Asiatic exaggeration,
by which she became still more grotesque
and tactless. In spite of her boasted ex-
clusiveness she had never quite learned to
understand the shades of foreign society,
and made frequent mistakes in her choice
of acquaintances.

Besides this, with all her weaknesses and
affectations, she was good natured to silli-
ness, and hospitable to prodigality.

" So early in the morning, Barbe—what a
surprise!" Natalie called to her, while she
tried not to let it be perceived how inoppor-

tune her sister's visit was to her just at
that moment. "That is charming, I must
introduce my husband to you."

"We know each other already, at least I
hope that Boris Nikolaivitch remembers me
—once in St. Petersburg, at the Olins. In
any case, I am very happy to renew the acquaintance," remarked the Jeliagin, and at
once reached him her fat little hand, in a
buckskin garden glove. Her voice was gut-
tural and rough, her whole face, as Lensky
could now see plainly, was painted.

"How are you, Nikolas?" She turned
to little Kolia, while she stroked his head in
a friendly manner. "Please greet a person,
or have I fallen as deeply in your displeasure as my Anna? I assure you that I cannot help it if she talks foolishly. Only
think, Boris Nikolaivitch, he cudgelled my
daughter Anna, day before yesterday, because she ventured to assert that a prince
was greater than a genius. He answered
her that not even an emperor was greater.
A genius came next to the dear God, and

as she would not agree to that, he struck
her, and hard."

The Jeliagin laughed. Lensky also
laughed involuntarily, but remarked in a
tone of admonition to his son, who had
shyly concealed himself behind his mother:
"A boy should never strike a girl; that is
not proper."

" But why did she say such foolish things?"
little Nikolas defended himself, while he
wrinkled his small forehead. " I cannot
bear that, and then she is larger than
I, so much "—he measured the width of his
hand above his head.

" She gave him quite a scratch, she was
not defenceless," said Barbara Alexandrovna, while she sat down and closed her um-
brella. " But to come to something more
interesting," she continued; "we have, in
spirit, followed you on every step of your
American triumphal march, Boris Nikolaivitch; the newspapers gave us the guide
thereto. I hope we will now see very much
of you. Natascha can tell you how well all

artists are received at our house,—and h'm!
—and if it is a question of a relation—*à
propos*, could you not come and dine with
us this evening? We are quite *entre nous*,
only Lis, Princess Zriny, that eccentric
Hungarian, Marinia Löwenskiold, a good
friend of yours, you remember her, a few
diplomats, etc. ; and we are bored as only
gens du monde are bored if they have been
together under the same roof for ten days.
Natalie can tell you how bored we are—
merely people from our coterie, who know
each other by heart; if you please. And
how stupid we are! ha, ha, ha! In desperation we arranged a race in the drawing-room
yesterday.   Arthur de Blincourt, while
jumping a barrier, dislocated a joint, and
now lies on a lounge, and lets himself be
looked after. But we all long for a new
element—*on vous attend comme le Messie*,
Boris Nikolaivitch. You will come, will
you not? We dine at eight o'clock."

While she chattered on with self-sat-
isfied fluency, it seemed to Boris as if

some one scratched a knife on a porcelain plate.

"Why does she roll her eyes so incessantly when she speaks? They do not look more beautiful when one sees so much of their orange-yellow whites," he thought to himself. Aloud he only remarked: "Do you really believe that I would amuse you better than a drawing-room race?"

"Ha, ha, ha!" laughed she. "That is splendid! I must repeat it to Marinia Löwenskiold, who raves about you. You will come, will you not?"

"No, I will not come," replied he sharply. "I do not feel myself equal to the task of amusing a dozen *gens du monde* who are bored."

"Well, as you will," said the Jeliagin, shrugging her shoulders. "Try to persuade him before evening, Natalie, and come, or send me word. I must go, we wish to ride out *en bande*, at eight. Adieu! Give me your hand, please, Kolia, and come and lunch with us. Anna will be pleased, and you shall have strawberries and whipped cream. Adieu!" With that she went away.

Lensky stared gloomily before him for a while, then he struck his clenched fist on the table so that all the dishes rattled: "From whence did this goose drop down so suddenly?" asked he.

"She lives in the castle in the park," said Natalie. "She has hired it for the summer."

"So!" grumbled Lensky. "Now if I had known that, I should never have thought of coming here."

"But I wrote you of it."

"Not a word."

"Certainly, in many letters; did you not have time to read them?"

Instead of replying to this, for him very unpleasant remark, Lensky said, in increasing rage: "Oh! now I understand the change which has taken place in you. She is horrible, your sister! For what does she hold me, that she takes this tone with me?"

"I cannot help her lack of tact," replied Natalie, gently and reproachfully.

"Ah, you are still influenced by your relations, by that narrow stupid crowd," he growled, crimson with rage. "You are condescending to me, yes, that is the right word, condescending, indulgent. Why do you start back from me when this silly machine comes near? Are you then ashamed of our love before her?"

"Our love!" repeated Natalie, with broken voice, strangely emphasizing the word "our."

He did not suspect anything from the trembling sadness of her voice, and did not once look at her.

Meanwhile he felt the anxious touch of a silky, soft child's hand. Little Kolia had come up to his father, and whispered to him shyly and pleadingly: "Papa, mamma is crying."

Lensky looked up, frightened. Yes, she had done her utmost to courageously smile through the unpleasant scene, but her over-excited nerves could not bear it; she sobbed convulsively.

"But Natalie, my angel, my little dove!" He could not see any woman weep, least of all his wife, whom he loved. He sprang up, took her in his arms, covered her eyes, her mouth, her whole face with kisses. "Do not torment yourself, my treasure! You are much, much too good to me; you are an angel! How could you ever take such a rough clown as I am? We are not suited to each other, Natascha."

"Oh, Boris! do you mean that?"

"Yes, I mean it," said he, gloomily. "Better, a hundred times better, would it have been for you if you had never seen me! You are so charming, so good, and I love you so idolatrously; but I am a fearful, a horrible man, and I cannot always govern myself—I cannot! I will yet torment you to death, my poor Natalie!" And he did not cease to caress and to kiss her.

Then she raised her head from his shoulder, and looking at him from eyes still shining with tears, with a glance full of tender fanaticism she said: "What does it matter, even if you kill me? it would still be beautiful! I would change with no woman in God's world, do you hear, with none! Think of what I have said to you to-day when one day you give me a last kiss in my coffin!"

.   .   .   .   .   .

Lensky could no longer get back into the old ways at home; however much he tried, he could not. As in the former year, only more significantly, more tormentingly, the feeling of growing discontent made itself felt in him. It seemed to him as if he could not remain for any length of time on the same spot; as if he must incessantly seek something which was no longer anywhere to be found.

For a couple of days he ill-humoredly stayed away from the castle, but when his brother-in-law paid him a visit and repeated the invitation of Barbara Alexandrovna in the most polite manner,—when one day, all the ladies staying at the castle as guests had come out in a body to give him an ovation—and especially when he had become immeasurably weary of the poetic monotony of life in the Hermitage ; he replied to Natalie, when she once asked him smilingly, with the intention of freeing him from his own constraining obstinacy, whether he thought it was really worth the trouble to longer play the bear: " No ! "

From that time, he passed every evening in the castle.

At first Natalie had been glad that the social intercourse there offered him a distraction. But soon the evenings in " Les Ormes " became a torment to her. The hateful change which had taken place in him during his long absence from his family, that change which Natalie had predicted, and by which she yet had been frightened at his return, as by something quite unexpected, never became more significant than during these evenings at the castle.

If, during the first years of his marriage,

through the lovely influence of his young wife, and especially through the wish to satisfy, to please her in everything, he had learned with quite incredible rapidity to follow the usual social customs of the country, and no longer to bear himself in the world as a genius, but as any other cultivated, well-bred man, he had completely forgotten it during his vagabond life, or rather it had become wearisome to him.

More than ever, his circle of action in a drawing-room limited itself to producing music and then being raved over by ladies. The incessant self-bewilderment in this smoke of incense how, where and whenever it might be, had become a necessity of existence for him. Everything in him had gone wild, even his art.

Together with a preference for perilous technical artifices, challenging musical unrestraint of every kind showed itself. Oftener than ever he fell into those mad moods in which he demanded things of his poor violin which it could not perform,

until it groaned and screamed as if in the
torments of hell, and if he had formerly complained that he could not govern himself,
he now boasted of it. It was his specialty,
by which he was distinguished from all the
virtuosos of his time. And, in spite of all
the underlying lack of restraint and the
impurity, that the sense-enslaving glow of
his art now unfolded stronger than before,
there could be no doubt. Especially over
the feminine portion of his listeners his
playing exercised a quite degrading charm.
The triumphs which he achieved in " Les
Ormes " proved this.

He profited by the situation. Although
it would have been tiresome to him to have
passed a whole evening among these people
of the world, far removed from all his most
intimate interests of life, without playing,
he sometimes let himself be urged almost
to lack of taste before he took up his violin. It happened once that he waited until
a particularly crazy enthusiast presented,
kneeling, his violin to him.

One of the musical ladies present sat down to the piano to accompany him; the others grouped themselves as near as possible round him, while they anxiously tried to express by their positions a kind of dying-away charm. He felt the longing glances of their eyes resting on him while he played. He saw the beautiful heads bent forward. It went to his head like a stunning oppression; he no longer knew himself. But they no longer knew themselves. If in the bearing of the great ladies who frequented his house in ————, in spite of all their enthusiasm for his art, there had still been a trace of patronage with reference to the artist, many of these beauties now fawned upon him like slaves who would sue for his favor.

When he had finished, no one of them knew by what special insanity she should over-trump the others, in order to prove to him her enthusiasm. And while the music-bewitched women crowded around him, to beg autographs or locks of hair from him, and carefully picked out the remains of his thrown-away cigarettes from the ash receiver, in order to keep them as relics, the Jeliagin told some new guest, in an adjoining room, the " romance of her sister," which she always concluded with the words : " My poor sister; so courted as she was ! You know that she refused Prince Truhetzkoi. We were inconsolable when we heard of her betrothal with Lensky. He is really a great genius !" And then she sighed.

But Natalie stood on the terrace which opened out of the music-room, quite alone. She was happy if she could remain alone, if no one came up to her to ask if she had a headache, or if anything else was the matter. Was anything the matter with her? No one could feel what she suffered, and there was also no human consolation which she would not have felt as an insult, however tenderly it was offered to her.

What were the little pin pricks which had excited her impatience in —————— to this pain !

Around her was the summer night, sultry
and still.   The black shadows of the trees
stretched themselves in the moonlight over
the gray-green turf on which not a single
dew-drop sparkled.

Out into the stillness of the night sounded
a loud, harsh laugh.   Natalie looked through
one of the flower-encircled windows into the
drawing-room.   There sat Lensky in a circle of ladies.

Heated by his wearying performance, he
wiped the perspiration from his temples,
from his neck.   He was relating something
that Natalie could not hear distinctly, but
which evidently seemed very droll to him,
and which convulsed his listeners; they
exhibited a kind of comically exaggerated
irritation.   An embarrassed smile appeared
on his lips, he seized the hand of the lady
who sat nearest to him, played with it
appeasingly, and drew it to his lips.   This
was his manner of making his apologies if
he had said something too racy.

Natalie stepped back in the shadow.   A

desperation, which was mingled with aversion, lay hold of her. Then, hollow, paining, quenching all the pleasure of life, quite like a physical discomfort, something crept over her which she would not explain to herself, which at no price would she have called by its name—jealousy.

.   .   .   .   .   .

The whole mud of his inner nature was stirred up as a stream highly swollen and unsettled after a wild storm, raving and foaming, tumbles in its bed, and can no longer find peace and rest therein.

From time to time he invited guests from Paris; sometimes they came uninvited. They usually remained to luncheon only, but Natalie had always time enough to be alarmed at them and to wish them away. They were no longer artistic celebrities like those whom Natalie had charmed to the " Hermitage" the year before; no, Lensky had reached that point in his career when an artist only tolerates courtiers and court fools about himself.

What a motley rabble that sometimes
was which assembled around him—artistic
Bohemians, freed from all social and moral
restraint !

The men usually remained to luncheon.
Natalie did her utmost to conceal the repul-
sion which the bearing and manner of expression of the throng caused her, even
from her husband. But sharp-sighted as he
was he guessed her feelings.

At first he tried to spare her; to keep
the conversation in suitable bounds as long
as she was present. But one day it became
too tiresome for him. Whether the wine
had gone to his head, or whether some
secret vexation irritated him, in any case he
felt the need of breaking his conventional
shackles. Scarcely had he given the sign
for excessive freedom of speech, when the
other men followed his lead. They laughed,
jested with Natalie and about her, without
the slightest consideration for her, as men
heated by wine do when they are together—
Lensky by far the worst among them all.

From time to time he looked at Natalie challengingly and angrily. Why was she so prudish? Why was she so affected? It was laughable in a married woman of her age— was nothing but foolishness and affectation.

At dessert she could bear it no longer; she left the table and locked herself in her room.

A kind of illness had come over her; she was near a swoon.

How painful the recollection of his roughness was to him later she knew nothing of. He was much too proud to let it be noticed. On the contrary, when he was with her again he acted as if he had a humor of hers to pardon.

From that time Natalie no longer appeared at these lunches. But in the distance she heard the rattling of glasses, the laughter.

She stopped her ears and bit her teeth into her lips.

.   .   .   .   .   .

With all this he became daily more out of temper and discontented.

At first his drawing-room triumphs in "Les Ormes" had amused him; gradually he lost the taste for them, found everything empty—childish. His position in the midst of this exclusive worldliness vexed him. While the women threw themselves at his head, he noticed a smile on the lips of the men which offended him. If, even at the beginning of his career, he had felt quite *à son aise* with the ladies of the aristocracy, he never, on the contrary, to the end of his life, learned to live in harmony with the men of that rank. Their treatment of him always remained objectionable to him. True, they always met him with the greatest politeness, but they never treated him as their equal, and were always a trifle too polite to him. If he entered the smoking-room while they, with hands in their pockets and cigars between their teeth, confidentially talked of politics, race-horses or ladies, the conversation immediately took a more earnest tone. As soon as he opened his mouth the others all listened in solemn silence; then one of them would leave the group, take him apart from the others, and try to talk of music with him. He embarrassed them and they embarrassed him.

Formerly, he had taken such things quite philosophically, but his sensitiveness had increased in recent times. In the long months which he had passed, going from city to city, winning triumphs and absolute, surrounded only by artists of the second and third class, he had gradually begun to feel himself the central point of the world. But here, in spite of the insane homage of the ladies, he very soon saw what a small *rôle* he really played on the world's stage, although he could give pleasure to so many by his art.

He could still tolerate the Russians, but sometimes strange diplomats came to the castle. The condescending flattery of these gentlemen was unbearable to him. What was he really in the eyes of these empty heads? he asked himself; an acrobat of the better sort, a man who existed merely for their accursed amusement. As if music were not the most beautiful of all arts, an art ten times holier, more God-like than the political, bungling work of these diplomats! "Art is the most enduring in the world. I am the only immortal among you all!" he said to himself. But then came the question: "Yes; am I then immortal? What have I accomplished up to this time to deserve artistic immortality?"

He only felt really happy on the days when all the men were occupied in hunting, and he and a handsome Spanish painter with a wooden leg were the only men in a circle of ten or twelve ladies, although, in his heart, the unmanliness of his position struck him bitterly enough.

.   .   .   .   .   .

The most charming of his admirers in "Les Ormes," the one who had decidedly taken the first place in his favor, was the Countess Marinia Löwenskiold. As already mentioned, she was a Pole, and married to a northern diplomat, from whom she lived separated, *à l'aimable.*

Naturally, she was an idealist, as almost all women are who have departed from the usual course in life. In addition, she was very musical. What was most piquant about her was the fact that, in spite of the separation from her husband, whom, besides, no one could bear, and in spite of her perilous coquetries, no one could say anything against her which could seriously injure her reputation.

Perhaps it was just this, her former haughty blamelessness, which attracted Lensky to her. She was very beautiful, she pleased him; and then—why did they say that this little Pole was invincible? He would see!

Among the guests in the castle was Count Leon Pachotin. Touchingly faithful to his old enthusiasm, he busied himself by singling out the wife of the virtuoso on every possible occasion, with the most exaggerated homage and attentions. He was still a very handsome man, was rich, had changed his military career, as is quite customary with young cavaliers, for that of diplomacy, in all appearances bid fair to reach the highest honors, and—was still unmarried. It was indescribably bitter to Natalie to play the humiliating *rôle* which had fallen to her in life, so near to him. Sometimes she felt his kind blue eyes resting upon her in sad compassion. Then the proud blood boiled within her. She collected herself in order that nothing might be noticed, and was again, so truly the charming, seductive, unapproachable Natalie Assanow of former days.

.   .   .   .   .   .

On a sultry evening, toward the middle of August, the company in the castle was unusually brilliant and numerous. The men and women sat in groups here and there in an immense pavilion—in which, by means of screens and thickets of flowers, all kinds of confidential nooks were formed —talked, laughed, coquetted, and sipped the refreshments which tall servants with solemn bearing and brilliant liveries presented.

Natalie had the consciousness this evening of looking particularly beautiful. Pachotin scarcely left her side. She observed that the count's manner to her irritated Lensky, that he looked over to her more than once uneasily, and she was glad and doubled her lovability to Pachotin.

Then she noticed that Boris had left the pavilion. With instinctive jealousy her eyes sought Countess Löwenskiold. She also was missing. Natalie's blood throbbed in every vein, she suddenly found Pachotin intrusive and awkward, wished to do nothing more speedily than to get rid of him.

"Please see if you can get me an ice, Count," she remarked. He rose obligingly. Scarcely had he left her when she stepped out from the pavilion on the terrace.

There was no one there, but out in the park, not very far, no further than a lady should permit herself to wander in the garden on a beautiful summer night in the company of a gentleman, she discovered two figures—he and she. A quite irresistible impulse drove her to follow them, to interrupt their conversation in some manner. Already she had taken a step forward, then, blushing for herself, she remained standing. Had it already gone so far with her that she should show herself capable of a degrading, pitiful act! She stood as if rooted to the ground. The pair in the park, yonder, also remained standing. She saw how Lensky stamped his foot, and threw back his brown head. She knew this despotic, violent movement. Then it seemed to her that she heard the words: "*pas de sens commun—enfantillages!*" Her heart beat violently, she turned away and reëntered the room. Soon after, Lensky joined the other guests, so did the Countess Löwenskiold. It did not escape Natalie that the latter entered the room by another door from him. The Polish woman was deathly pale, and her lips burned with fever. In Lensky's manner, on the contrary, not a trace of excitement betrayed itself; he was even more lovable than usual, and polite to all the ladies, and without being specially urged, took up his violin.

While he played, he turned away from the Löwenskiold, and he charmed such tones from his Amati that evening, tones of such touching, painful sweetness, that the most earnest men present, with the women, bowed before his art.

While he played, the nervous countess was seized with a fit of weeping, and left the room.

A little later, Natalie and Lensky walked home together through the park. The way which they took was enclosed on both sides by thick bushes, which almost met over their heads in a transparent arch. The moonbeams slid through the branches, and the shadows of the leaves spread themselves out like ghostly lace-work over the yellow gravel. An oppressive sultriness, the breathless, sticky sultriness of the old heat of the day, which remained hanging in the thicket, made breathing difficult.

Neither of them spoke a word. But while she, holding her head very high in the air, looked straight before her, his glance rested ever more frequently on her. In accordance with the custom which ruled in the castle, she wore evening dress, and, on account of the heat, had let the white, gold-embroidered burnous slip down a little from her bare shoulders. The moonlight shone on her neck. She held her little head somewhat averted. In vain he tried to look in her eyes; he only saw the outline of her cheek, her chin, and neck; but how charming all that was! Never before, since his return, had she pleased him so. It really was worth the pains to only look at another woman near this one. Giving way to a sudden excitement, mingled with remorse, he drew her to him and pressed his lips to her shoulder. But she escaped his embrace, not without a certain correcting roughness. His arms fell loosely at his sides, but he could not remove his gaze from her. How high she held her head, what annihilating arrogance her little mouth expressed! In his mind he saw Pachotin bent over her chair, humbly intent on the slightest sign of her favor.

Who knows? perhaps she regrets, thought he to himself, and a furious rage gnawed at his heart.

.   .   .   .   .   .

About three days after this scene—three days, during which Natalie and Lensky had lived together in mutual wrath, without speaking a word to each other, Lensky told his wife he must to-day go to Paris, in order to arrange with Flaxland the publication of one of his works; at the same time he wished to make use of the opportunity to see and hear Gounod's new opera. He could, therefore, only come home the next day on the five o'clock train. He said all that in a very grumbling tone, did not give her a kiss for farewell, and immediately went to the railroad.

She fancied him already far away, when he returned again. "Have you forgotten anything?" she asked him.

"Yes; namely, I would like to know if you perhaps have anything to be done in Paris—and then—if you wish, you can come with me; we will go to the opera together. I will wait, as far as I am concerned, for the next train, so that there will be time enough for you to make ready."

If he had only said that pleasantly, but he said it roughly, disagreeably, as if it did not concern him at all. He had offended Natalie too much recently for her to agree with his first attempt at reconciliation.

"I thank you very much," she replied coldly; "you will amuse yourself much better without me."

For one moment he hesitated; then he shrugged his shoulders and went.

Scarcely had he gone when Natalie was

overcome with remorse for her stubbornness
and obstinacy.

Truly it was unwise and hateful not to
come to meet him, if he, proud as he was,
took the first step. She could have cried
from anger with herself. A true child, as
in the bottom of her heart she still was, she
could not cease to think of the pleasure
which she so petulantly had renounced.
How charming it would have been to pass
a whole day alone with him in Paris. To
dine in the Café Anglais, very quickly and
quite early, so as not to miss the opera,
but still very excellently; she even made
out the *menu*—ah! she knew all his favorite
dishes so well; then the next day they
would have bought all kinds of useless,
pretty things together. She knew, from
former years, how good-naturedly and patiently he would let himself be dragged in
the great bazaars. She would have bought
Kolia playthings and baby an embroidered
dress—she saw the little dress before her—
and instead of all that—ah, how vexatious!

The hours dragged slowly; she scarcely put her foot out of the house. She also remained at home in the evening; the castle had really no power of attraction for her. When Kolia took the place opposite her at dinner, and unfolded his napkin with an important air, he remarked: "See, mamma, now it is just like the day after papa had gone away to America, only you are not so sad, because you know that he is coming back soon."

Natalie smiled at the child. After awhile Kolia began anew:

"Mamma, shall we go to meet papa to-morrow?"

She nodded.

Kolia rested his little head thoughtfully on his hand.

"I wonder if he will miss the train again?" said he.

.　　　.　　　.　　　.　　　.　　　.

In accordance with a loving agreement, Natalie had formerly been the only one who possessed the right to move anything in Lensky's sanctum, and to remove the dust from his writing-table. With devoted punctuality she had always performed this task. Only very recently had she been untrue to this dear custom. But this time he should observe, as soon as he returned, that she had busied herself for him during his absence.

She was in an optimistic frame of mind. She would no longer be angry with him because he of late had caused her so many bitter hours. He himself had not been happy. He was not yet really acclimatized at home. She had known that she must first win him back again after his long absence. Why had she from exaggerated pride so soon crossed arms? To remember the low expressions which he sometimes now made use of, and especially in company with the motley crowd that came over to him from Paris, this really sent the blood to her cheeks—but still he had scarcely known what he said. She had needlessly irritated him by her childish prudery ; one must take these great natures, always in-

clined to exaggeration, as they were, and
not make them obstinate by quite uselessly
checking and restraining them.

Only at the thought of the Countess
Löwenskiold an unpleasant shudder ran
over her.   And suddenly the thought
flashed through her: "What does he really wish in Paris?"   But almost laughingly
she answered herself: "As if he could wish
anything evil when he asked me to accompany him!"

After she had carefully and daintily set
everything to rights on the writing-table,
she went down in the garden to cut for it the
most beautiful roses which she could find.

Softly humming one of the songs which
he had dedicated to her as bride, she carried
the flowers, tastefully arranged in a vase,
into his room, and placed them on his writing-table.   There she discovered in a brass
ash receiver a half-burned paper which had
formerly escaped her.   She looked at the
paper to see whether she might throw it
away.   Her heart stood still.   She read the

words written in French: "O thou my creator, my redeemer—my ruiner—broken —Paris." The rest of the lines were burned.

She could scarcely stand. From whom were these lines? was not that the writing of Countess Löwenskiold? No, no, it was not possible—he asked me to accompany him. Yes, he asked me to accompany him. She repeated it ten times, a hundred times, in order to shake off from herself the conviction that began so pitilessly to weigh down upon her. She could not believe such a thing, she would not. Countess Löwenskiold had certainly not left " Les Ormes "!

But, however she fights with her distrust, she cannot overcome it. A thousand little particulars occur to her.

The sun shines down hot and full from the sapphire-blue heaven. Natalie does not trouble herself about that; straight through the park she hurries, without parasol, without hat, over to the castle. She will inform herself with as little risk as possible. There is no one at home; the ladies

17

have not yet returned from a walk. What a shame! "*La princesse regrettera beaucoup,*" remarked the *maître d'hôtel*, who had received her in the entrance-hall. " Perhaps madame will remain to lunch; they will lay a place for madame."

He is an old acquaintance, a servant whom Natalie has known for years. "Oh, no; I cannot stay; I only wished to inquire after the health of the Countess Löwenskiold; she has looked so miserable of late," murmured she.

" Madame la Comtesse Löwenskiold?" says the man, astonished. "Ah! she is no longer here. The poor countess left day before yesterday evening, quite unexpectedly. It occurred to me that she looked very badly. Did madame also notice it?"

What she stammered in answer to his question she does not know. A few minutes later she hurries homeward again through the park, hatless, parasolless. The sun still beams down full and golden upon the earth from the sapphire sky. She does

not feel the burning of the sun, and does
not see that the sky is blue. For her the
sun is dead and the sky black. It seems to
her that .it sinks slowly down upon her,
heavy and breath-robbing, like a sultry,
bruising weight.

"He wished to take me with him," she
still repeats, as if the words held consolation; "yes, he wished to take me with
him." Then she remembers the embarrassed, uneasy expression which his face
wore when he returned at the last minute
to ask her to accompany him. Evidently
he had had a fit of remorse.

"I could have prevented it," she murmured, with hollow voice. Then she shook
in her whole body with rage and horror.

. . . . . .

About this time, gloomily looking before
him, Lensky went through the Rue de la
Paix. He did not know why he went along
this street rather than another. It was
quite indifferent to him where he was; he
only wished to kill time. A furious anger

with himself shook him; at the same time
disgust tormented him. It was always the
same; one woman was just like the others.
The only one who was different was his
own wife; and he—well, he had taken the
first slight opportunity to insult her.

He came by the hotel in which he had
lived with her the former year. He hastened his steps. From a jeweller's shop the
most wonderful jewels sparkled at him. He
entered. He would take something to
Natalie; would give her a little pleasure.
He purchased a pretty pin set with emeralds. She had a preference for emeralds.
Scarcely had he left the shop when it
seemed to him that the little case in his
pocket weighed upon him, pulled him down
to the ground. How had he dared venture
to offer her a gift in this moment! He
took the little case and threw it on the
ground—trod on it, once, twice, raging, beside himself. So! that did him good. He
must vent his wrath in some way.

.   .   .   .   .   .

When he returned home about five o'clock, he was calmer. What had happened could not be changed, it was now only worth while not to ruin the future. It disquieted him that Natalie did not meet him, but after all, he was not very astonished. She still felt a little vexed with him. He would soon make an end of that. He asked where she was. " In her room," they told him. But what was that? Everything was upturned, chests stood open, on chairs and tables lay piles of linen, clothes, as before a departure. He did not yet understand, but still he noticed that she started violently at his entrance, without looking around at him.

" What are you doing, Natalie? Are you preparing for departure?" asked he.

" As you see," replied she shortly, and continued her strange occupation.

" It is a good idea," said he. " I already myself wished to make the proposition to you to move away from here. But how did you really come to think of it?"

Instead of any answer, she merely shrugged her shoulders. A short pause followed.

He stepped somewhat nearer to her. "Natalie," said he, earnestly, warmly and gently, with his old, dear voice, the voice which always went so deep to her heart, and which she now heard again for the first time since his return from America, "Natalie, do you not think that we would do better to make peace with each other?"

He wished to put his arm round her, but she repulsed him. In so doing, for the first time she turned her face to him. With horror he perceived how miserable she looked.

Her lips were pale, her features sharpened like a dead person's. For one moment she still restrained herself, her eyes sought his. An unrest, a hope fevered in her. "Perhaps I have in vain martyred and tormented myself," she said to herself. "He certainly could not speak so to me, if——"

With trembling hand she opened a little box, and took out the half-singed letter which she had not been able to overcome herself from carrying about with her. She handed Lensky the letter.

He changed color. "What accident has played this silly note into your hands?" he burst out.

"No matter about that," she replied dully, and with that she tottered so that she must catch hold of a chair so as not to fall. "Were you—in company—with the Löwenskiold—in Paris—or—not?"

Why could he not lie? He remained silent.

Once more she looked at him, despairingly and supplicatingly. He turned away his head.

She gave a gasping cry, pushed back the hair from her temples with both hands, and sank in a chair. Then she pointed with her pale, trembling hand to the door.

Lensky did not move.

"Go!" said she, severely; and her hand no longer trembled, and her gesture was more imperious, more proud.

Instead of obeying her command, he sank down at her feet and covered the hem of her dress with kisses. "I have sinned against you," he said; "yes, but if you knew how furious I am with myself, and how little my heart was concerned in the affair, you would pardon me. You will not certainly be jealous of something that is quite beneath one's notice; one does not always think immediately what one is doing." He shrugged his shoulders impatiently. "For this reason you are still the only woman in the world for me. Really, my angel, it is not worth the pains that you should torment yourself!" He took her hand in his.

But she started back from his touch. "Leave me!" said she, violently. "All is at an end between us—go!"

For the first time he comprehended the gravity of the situation. "All at an end—" he murmured, while he rose. "What do you mean?"

"That I will no longer bear to be under

the same roof with you; that I will go back
to my mother; that I insist upon a separation—that is what I mean. Did you, then,
expect anything different?"

He clutched his forehead. "A separation! but that is impossible!" he gasped.
"A separation—the children!"

She started. "Yes—the children!" murmured she, dully, inconsolably; "the children!" And with a bitter smile she looked
down on her preparations for the journey,
on the trunks, the effects lying about.

Then he once more stepped up to her.
"You see that the bond between us can
never more be broken," said he, gently.
"You cannot go!"

"No!" said she harshly. "No, I cannot
go—not even that consolation remains to
me. As the mother of your children I must
remain under your roof. But in everything
else—between me and you all is at an end.
Go!"

He went.

.   .   .   .   .   .

He betook himself to his study. Scarcely had he entered here when a peculiar feeling of mingled emotion and anxiety came over him. He noticed that she had been here, noticed that she had everywhere removed the dust ; that she had arranged his of late neglected writing-table, and how understandingly, with what loving consideration of all his whims! He noticed the vase with fresh roses. Evidently she had busied herself for him during his absence. She had wished to be reconciled to him, and while she troubled herself for him she must have found the note somewhere in this room. "It is all over," he told himself ; "but that is really not possible. It is jealousy that speaks from her ; that will pass away." Jealousy! Yes, if it had really only been jealousy, but that which he had read in her features was something else—almost a kind of loathing. What, then, had he done? He had left a distinguished young woman, beautiful as a picture, alone for eight months, and when he returned, instead of recompensing her for her long, sad loneliness by loving consideration, he had daily, before her eyes, let himself be raved over by other women, and at last——

"She despises me, and she is right!" he murmured to himself. "If she had borne this also, she would have been pitiable, and I must have despised her like the others—she, my proud, splendid Natalie!"

He sat at his writing-table, and rested his head in his hand.

The twilight shadows spread over the floor, and slid down from the ceiling, and made the corners of the room invisible, and obliterated the outlines of the furniture. The colors died; only the white roses shone in a ghostly manner in the half light.

Then the door opened; the servant announced that dinner was served.

It seemed strange to him that he should go to the table to-day as any other day; it was not possible for him to eat anything, but he was ashamed to cause talk among the servants, and so he went into the din-

ing-room. "Will she be there?" he asked
himself. How could he have even fancied
such a thing? Naturally she was missing.
Only Kolia was there, and stood expect-
antly near the silver soup tureen, which
shone on the table. In their little family
circle, Lensky always himself served the
soup. Kolia had raised himself on tiptoes,
and with one slender finger had pushed the
cover of the dish somewhat to one side.
He stretched his little nose eagerly forward,
and slowly inhaled the rising odor, while
with a deliciously old, wise connoisseur expression he drew down his nostrils and
closed his eyes.

"I see already, it is crab soup—my favorite soup, papa!" he remarked, and then
with agility he climbed up on the chair,
which, on account of his still insufficient
stature, was prepared with a cushion for
him.

It was certainly only a quite trivial little
affair, and yet it stabbed Lensky to the
heart.

Potage au bisque was also his favorite soup. He stared at Natalie's place, which remained vacant.

A great embarrassment mingled with his pain. He sent the servant, busy at the side-board, out of the room on some pre-text.

"Mother is not coming?" he turned to the boy, who had already begun to eat his soup.

"No; mamma has a headache. Poor mamma!"

"Do you wish to be a very clever boy, Kolia?"

"Yes, papa!"

"Then take this bowl of soup to your mother. Do not spill it; perhaps mamma will take a few drops."

With an important face Kolia undertook his errand. Lensky opened the door of the dining-room for him, and looked after him while he tripped along the green-carpeted, dimly-lighted corridor. How pretty and pleasing all that was! The lamps, which stood out from old-fashioned inlaid plates of polished copper, the stags' antlers on the brown wainscoting. And he had not felt happy at home!

Then Kolia came springing back. " I left the soup there," he told his father, who had remained listening and spying in the doorway, " but mamma did not wish to eat it."

" What is mamma doing ? "

" She is holding little sister on her lap."

In the course of the meal, and when he noticed that his father's plate continually remained empty, Kolia also lost his appetite. At first, in the most caressing tones, he urged his father to eat.

" But, papa, don't you see, you must help yourself to a little bit ; it is such a good dinner to-day. We made out the bill of fare, mamma and I, early this morning at breakfast, and I remembered all your favorite dishes which she had forgotten. She was so gay to-day, before she had a headache, and she only got that headache because she ran through the park to-day without any hat, in the noon sun. But eat something, papa."

Lensky still stared at Natalie's empty place.

All at once he noticed an unusual commotion in the house; confused talking together, quick running to and fro. He sprang up and went out in the corridor.

There he saw Natalie's maid, with disturbed face, and anxious, over-hasty steps, coming out of her mistress' room.

"What is the matter; is madame more ill?" he asked in sudden fright.

"No, monsieur, but the little girl is very ill; it came on quite suddenly. Madame has told me to hurry over to Chancy for the doctor."

For one moment he stood still; then he turned to the sick-room—entered.

.   .   .   .   .   .

It was no contagious illness. Kolia was not sent away from the house; only they told him to keep very quiet, for which he was ready without that, for the weight which oppressed the house was sufficient to constrain the fresh animation of his elastic child-nature. Quite cautiously he only occasionally crept up to the sick-room, opened the door, whose knob he could scarcely reach with his little hand, and whispered: " How is little sister now? "

Yes, how was the little sister?

It was an inflammation of the lungs which had attacked the little one. The physician did not conceal from the parents what little hope there was of recovery.

Two days, three nights long, they both sat together near the cradle in which the sick little girl lay ; two days, three nights, in which the tiny body restlessly threw itself here and there between the lace-trimmed pillows, while the breath, interrupted by fierce and tormenting fits of coughing, with difficulty gaspingly forced itself out from the little breast. Sometimes Maschenka cried impatiently and pulled at the coverings with her weak little hands, and then looked at her parents with that hurt, reproachful look with which quite little children desire relief from their parents.

Why did not her parents help her—why must she suffer so?

And Natalie, who formerly had been the tenderest mother in the whole world, took this all wearily, almost indifferently, as a person whose heart, benumbed by a great despair, is no longer susceptible to a new pain. She scarcely worried herself over the endangered little life. Yes! Maschenka would die, she told herself, the dear, charming Maschenka, over whom she had always so rejoiced. She still heard her cooing laughter like a distant echo in her remembrance. Yes, Maschenka would die! Why should she not die? It was really better for her than to grow up to feel such grief in the future as had burned and parched her mother's heart. Yes, she would die, and then Natalie would lay her head down on the little pillow, near the pale face of the

child, and fall asleep forever—rest—forget !
When Maschenka was dead, Natalie had no
more duties !— Kolia?—Oh, Kolia would
make his way in the world.

But Maschenka did not wish to die : this
world pleased her too well, she did not
wish to.

The fever became higher; ever more impatiently the child threw herself about in
the cradle. On the evening of the third
day the doctor, a skilful, wise, conscientious family physician, whom Natalie had
frequently consulted for any little illness of
the children, and who, under the direction
of a Parisian specialist, fought with death
for Maschenka's little life,—on the evening
of the third day he said that probably the
crisis would occur in the night; he would
come again at six o'clock in the morning
and look after it. He said that very sadly.
Lensky accompanied him out. When he
came back in the sick-room, the expression
of his face was still sadder than before.

The little one became still more restless

—she would not stay in her cradle. Incessantly she raised herself from the pillows, cried pitifully, and stretched out her little arms. Natalie took the little patient, warmly wrapped in coverings, on her lap, but the little one would not stay there either. She felt that her mother was not just the same to her as formerly. Quite angrily she turned away from her, and stretched out her little hands to her father. Lensky took her in his arms, wrapped the covering still closer round her tiny limbs, and with a thousand tender words, coaxed her to rest. With what evident pleasure the little body leaned against his breast!

Natalie's eyes rested on him. It had been just the same for two days. He had cared for the child, not she. Only she now, for the first time, took account of it. How tenderly he held the child! what touchingly poetic words of love he whispered to it! Expressions, such as one finds only in those songs in which the people complain of their pain! Just such words had he formerly found for her—at that time—in those old days, when he still loved her—and a stream of new, animating warmth crept through her benumbed heart.

She still watched him. Her eyelids became heavy.

Suddenly she started up, looked confusedly about her; she had been fast asleep. What had happened meanwhile? The morning light already streamed into the room; without the rain rattled against the window panes. When had it begun to rain then? Where was **Lensky?** He stood near the window and gazed **out.** How sad he looked, how pale!

The child!—and with a feeling of immeasurably painful anxiety her heart now fully awoke to new life. She had not the courage to look in the cradle. Then Lensky turned to her. "The child!" murmured she.

He laid his finger on his mouth. "She sleeps—" Then listening: "The doctor comes."

The physician entered. He bent over the cradle; the little patient slept calmly and sweetly, her little fist against her cheek. Her little face was very pale and sadly lengthened, but her brow was moist and a peaceful expression was on her tiny mouth.

"She is better," said the doctor, astonished and pleased. He scarcely understood it. "The fever is gone, the crisis is past, and if there are no quite unusual circumstances, the danger is over. A couple of spoonfuls of strong broth when she wakes, and no more medicine. Adieu, *à tantôt!*" and he left the room.

The door had closed behind him, his steps resounded in the corridor. Natalie rose; she did not know what she wished; to look at the child, to fall on her knees, to pray! Then her eyes met Lensky's. She started, stretched out her arms as if to repel a suddenly awakened pain—a swoon overcame her—she sank down. He took her in his arms, carried her into the adjoining room, and stretched her out on a couch. He opened the window and let the spicy, rain-cooled morning air stream in. Then he wet the temples of the unconscious woman with cologne and loosened her dress. At that her only carelessly fastened-up hair loosed itself and slid down in all its dark abundance over her shoulders.

How wonderfully charming she looked in her pale, melancholy loveliness! Involuntarily he approached his lips to her temples; then she opened her eyes; a shudder shook her frame and she turned her face away from him.

It went through him from the top of his head to the sole of his foot. He had forgotten, but now he remembered accurately. How dared he approach this woman so confidentially!—she was no longer his wife. She had only tolerated him near her as long as the child lay sick, really only tolerated! With fearful bitterness he remembered how she had held herself far from him, even near Maschenka's bed of pain. And now, when the little one was well—

why let himself be shown the door a second time?

"You need not be afraid, Natalie, I am going; I had only forgotten—pardon!" With that he could not deny himself to take her hand; he believed she would draw away her hand from him; no, she let it lie quite passively in his. Now he wished to free it, but then, quite softly, but ever firmer, her fingers closed round his. She herself held him back. Rejoicing and sobbing he drew her to his breast.

Scarcely a moment later he felt in his inmost heart quite strangely, uncomprehendingly, a cold gnawing vexation.

He did not understand that she could pardon so easily. He had not expected that of her.

FOURTH BOOK.

DEAR NATALIE!—Owing to business affairs which
will claim me still longer, it will be impossible for
me to come to Trouville before the beginning of September. I am very sorry, but I hope and wish that
you will not, on this account, put off your journey to
the sea-shore; you know how you need the stay in
the bracing air. I have engaged a residence for you
through Madame de C., and also had everything
arranged for your comfortable reception—a low
châlet with a look-out over the sea. I know how you
love it,—the poor wild sea, that cannot help it if it
sometimes crushes a ship, and that finds no rest from
despair over the evil which it does and cannot
prevent.

You must not take any sea-baths; Dr. H. suitably
impressed that upon me in the spring. But in any
case, wait until I come.

From my great, clever boy I often receive long,
pretty, regularly written letters which please me
very much. I will show them to you when we are

together again. The boy is romantic, through and
through, which touches me in these our present
times, and also a little of a pedant, which makes me
impatient, but still, he is a dear, splendid fellow, and
that you must tell him from me.

The little note, which I recently received from
Maschenka, was laughably comic, and sweet enough
to eat. The little witch wrote me quite secretly,
without telling you anything about it. She confessed
all her naughtinesses to me very remorsefully and
over hurriedly, from anxiety that you might write
something about them to me. Is she really so
naughty, and passionate, and wild? She is still
charming in spite of all, so thoroughly good-hearted
and tender and generous, and withal so incredibly
gifted. I tell you her little note—it was adorned
with three ink spots, and I could not read a word of
the writing—but still it was a little poem.

And how she loves you! Just as she is, I find
her charming enough to make one lose one's head
over her; and I am very sorry that one must cure
her of her amusing little faults; they are so becoming to her. That you must naturally not tell her
from me, but give her a very warm kiss from me on
her full, defiant lips, of which you always assert that
they are like mine. Do not vex yourself too much
over it, — rejoice in our little gypsy as she is.

And if you again worry over her inherited good-for-nothingness, then look in her wonderfully beautiful, large eyes, which she did not inherit from me. You will find your soul in them—let that be your consolation. Farewell, my angel, spare yourself really—really! Only do not think of saving at all on the journey. You know that I cannot bear that. Think only of your comfort and of what a joy it would be to me if, at our next meeting, I should find your poor thin cheeks somewhat rounder than when I left you.

Your boundlessly devoted

BORIS.

It is in Berlin, in the Hôtel du Nord, nine years after the first violent quarrel, the first passionate reconciliation with her husband, that Natalie receives this letter.

She had left St. Petersburg a few days before, in order, as by agreement, to meet Lensky, whom she has not seen since the beginning of March, in the German capital. It had been a great disappointment for her that she had not found Boris in Berlin, but he has accustomed her to disappointments.

She reads the letter once more. It is a

dear, good letter. Ah! Natalie has received such dear, good, tender letters from all the large cities in Europe and America—and knows———

Not that Boris is deceiving her when he writes to her in this tender tone. No, every trace of falseness is strange to him, his attachment to her, his anxiety about her, are sincere—but———

What use to grieve over it? These great geniuses are never different. One must not judge them like other men! With this shallow commonplace, with which she has so often put to sleep her inconsolable heart if it sometimes wishes violently to rise up against its oppressive, ignominious lot, she compels it to rest again to-day. It is easier now than formerly; her poor heart has already accustomed itself to grievances.

Nine years have passed since that time in the pretty, cosey Hermitage when she— forgave him too easily, and thereby lost her power over him forever. She has known it a long time. Late in that following autumn

a great symphony by him was given in the
"Gewandhaus," in Leipzig. The work was
beautiful, the success moderate, Lensky's
discouragement exaggerated, quite morbid.
A few months later he took up his wander-
er's staff anew, and left Petersburg, where
he had returned with his family, in order to
distract himself by the most exaggerated
virtuoso triumphs from the humiliation
which had befallen the composer. Oftener,
ever oftener, he had then left wife and children, and now, in his own house, he had
long been only an indulged, distinguished
guest.

But in the time which he every year
devoted to his wife, to his family, he behaved
in an exemplary fashion. He did everything that lay in his power to make life
bearable to Natalie—everything except to
lay a restraint upon himself ; that he simply
could not, and for that reason he must
leave home so often in order to vent his
passion.

Natalie's nature was broken. An unexpressed, numbing, blunting conviction that this was the natural course of things, and that nothing of all this could be changed, had overpowered her. As to what might take place while he was away from her, of that she did not permit herself to think.

With his art matters had long gone downward, even more rapidly than Natalie—who already after his return from America had been startled by the exaggerations to which he had accustomed himself in his playing—had deemed possible. At that time he had given the reins to his temperament with assiduity in order to dazzle the public. Now—now, he had long lost power over himself. And concerning his compositions ! A fearful pain contracted Natalie's heart if she thought how she had formerly, in her tender enthusiasm, called him the last musical poet, in opposition to the other great composers of modern times, whom at that time she had described as—musical bunglers. She could no longer remember the speech without blushing.

The bunglers had all grown above his head. One scarcely spoke of his compositions now, and the worst of it was— Natalie herself no longer cared to hear them.

Where was the sweet, sunny, charming element of his first little works? Where the fiery earnestness, the penetrating, noble sound of pain in his later works?

Sleepy monotony, noisy emptiness were now the characteristics of his musical creations. Certainly, here and there appeared melodies of wonderful beauty; but who had the patience to seek out the lovely oases in this sterile musical wilderness?

Once, Natalie had hesitatingly made a remark to him about a new composition. But he, who had formerly showed himself of such unimpeachable gentleness toward her, had flown into a passion, and had even for many days remained irritable. Since that time she said nothing more, but let him have his way, as she let him have his way in everything, only that she might not break the last thin thread which still held them together.

.   .   .   .   .   .

She had read the letter a third time. " Business affairs detain him," she murmured to herself. " Business affairs! He writes from Leipzig; why does he not ask me to come to him?" She shrugged her shoulders—what good to think of it?

Suddenly her cheeks burned, her breath came short. She pours out a glass of water, throws a couple of bits of ice from a porcelain bowl in it, and drinks thirstily. " Such great geniuses are never different," she says to herself again. She begins to walk up and down in the room uneasily. At last she goes to the window and looks out.

A great weariness lay over everything. The lindens slept, wrapped in white dust; the stony heroes at their feet looked morose and weary, as if they were satiated with letting themselves parch on their pedestals. They throw pitch-black shadows over the

sun-burned road. A black poodle lies at
the foot of one of the memorials, on its
back, and does its utmost to pull off the
muzzle on its nose. The people are weary
and pale, and crowd into the shadow wherever they can. Everything flees the sun.
No one remembers another such hot, dry,
oppressive summer. And suddenly a
strange longing for shade comes over
Natalie ; for some deep, cool, shady place
in which she can rest.

The hollow, oppressive feeling about her
heart has become more significant, has
taken, at length, the form of a piercing
physical pain. She lays her hand on her
breast ; the physicians have told her that
she should spare herself, should guard
against every vehement sensation, because
her heart is affected. Suddenly she breaks
out in convulsive sobbing. Spare herself !
Is it worth the trouble to spare one's self ;
to exert one's self for the preservation of
this poor life ; is it worth the trouble to
bend down again and again in the mire for

the poor little bit of happiness that is thrown to one as an alms?

Then the door opens; a charming little girl of about ten years, large-eyed, gay, with wonderful curly hair hanging far down her back, with very long black stockings and very short white dress, hops in—Maschenka, who had been to walk with the maid. The first thing which she discovers when she has scarcely greeted her mother and given her a somewhat breathless and hurried account of the various impressions she has formed on her walk, is Lensky's letter, which has remained lying on the table. "Oh, from papa!" says she. "When is he coming; to-morrow?" and her eyes shine.

"He is not coming; we are going to Trouville without him," replies Natalie, wearily.

"Without him," repeats Maschenka; her sweet, large-eyed cherub's face lengthens. "Oh!"—looking at Natalie attentively— "Did you cry over that, mamma?"

Natalie says nothing, only turns her head away with a gesture of displeasure.

" He is coming after us?" asks Maschenka, embarrassed.

" He promises to," replies Natalie, with difficultly restrained bitterness.

" Poor mamma!" and Maschenka tenderly kisses the tears away from her mother's cheek. " You must not cry, it is not good for you. You know papa cannot bear to see you cry."

It is quite inexplicable how nature has been able to bestow upon this tender, childish, velvet-cheeked little being such a striking likeness to the face stamped by time, weather, and life of the virtuoso. The troubled, strangely deep look with which Maschenka regards her mother ; the tender and still defiant expression of her full lips ; the manner of drawing together her delicate brows, all that reminds one of her father. But that in which her likeness to him is most strikingly announced, is the bewitching heartiness of her manner, the flattering insinuation of her caresses.

Natalie observes her with quite fixed attention, then draws her to her and kisses her passionately on both eyes.

Meanwhile there is a knock at the door. It is a waiter, who brings a telegram from Petersburg. Natalie starts, her thoughts fly to her son whom she has left behind them. But no—the telegram has nothing to do with Kolia. It is really not from Petersburg, but has only sought her there, and has been sent after her to Berlin. She reads:

DRESDEN, HÔTEL BELLEVUE, *August 4th.*
Can you not take the roundabout way through Dresden? We would be very glad to see you.
SERGEI.

Why should she not take the roundabout way through Dresden? Why should she hasten to reach Trouville, the full, empty Trouville, where no one will be glad to see her?

. . . . . .

Shortly after his reconciliation with his sister, Sergei had left St. Petersburg, in order to follow his brilliant but exacting diplomatic wandering career from one important but remote post to another, and now he had at length been recalled to Petersburg, to fill a high position at home. Natalie cherished the conviction that he suspected nothing of the slow crumbling together of her happiness. How should he! Before him, more than before all the others, she had concealed her great inconsolableness. In the long letter which, by agreement, she wrote him every month, she had always forced herself to take as gay as possible a tone, and even if she was accustomed, in the description of her "domestic happiness" to dwell at especial length on the lovability and happy dispositions of both of her children, she yet had never failed to mention the goodness of their father and his unwearied consideration for her. "How he would triumph if he knew!" she said to herself, on the platform in Dresden, while she uneasily looked round for her brother, whom she had informed by telegram of the hour of her arrival. "If he knew anything of it!" she said to herself, and at the mere thought, it seemed to her that she would flee to the end of the world, rather than bear the cold scrutinizing glance of his eye. Then a very slender man in blameless English clothes came up to her, looked at her a moment uncertainly, put up his eye-glass—"Natalie! it is really you!" and evidently truly pleased to see her again he draws her hand to his lips. And now she is also glad to see him, is pleased to be with her brother, as she has never yet been glad since her betrothal to Lensky. He has changed very much since that time in Rome when he had vainly sought to destroy Natalie's illusions; but, as with all really distinguished men, growing old was becoming to him. If his bearing is still proud, it has yet lost much of its harsh, nervous, immature arrogance of that time. His fine features are still sharper, but his glance has become softer, more benevolent.

"That is your little girl?" says he, bending down to Maschenka, pleasantly. "May one ask a kiss of such a large young lady?"

The gay Maschenka, always bent upon the conquest of all hearts, hops up to him with hearty readiness, and throws both her little arms round his neck. "*Elle est charmante!*" whispers Sergei in a somewhat patronizing tone to Natalie.

"We find her very like the Maria Ægyptica of Ribera—your favorite picture in the Dresden Gallery. Do you not remember it?"

"Indeed!" The prince bends down a second time, wonderingly, to Maschenka. Suddenly his face takes on a discontented expression. "She chiefly resembles Lensky; I do not understand how that could escape me!" says he, and his tone expresses decided displeasure.

"And still if he knew!" thinks Natalie.

"Kolia looks like you," says she, hastily.

"They have often written me that," says the prince. "Besides, they tell me only good things of him; I shall be glad to see a great deal of him in Petersburg. And now come, Natalie. I wished to have rooms in Bellevue for you, but there were none to be had; not a mouse hole; all engaged. We ourselves live at the extreme end of a corridor. So I have taken a little apartment for you in the Hôtel du Saxe. It is a plain house, but the nearest one to us, and you will not be there much. Send your maid ahead with the luggage. I hope you will now come direct to our rooms with me, you and the little one; my wife awaits you at dinner."

.   .   .   .   .   .

And now Natalie has been in Dresden since many hours. The joy of the meeting with her brother has fled, a great depression benumbs her whole being. What a home! Sergei's wife, born a Countess Brok, who is two years older than he, and whom he has married on account of the influential position of her father, suffers with rheumatism, on which account she fears a little bit of too warm sunshine as well as a slight draught.

The meal is taken in the drawing-room of
the married pair, instead of down on the
gay, sunny terrace, as Sergei had ordered.
After the princess has welcomed Natalie,
and has said something in praise of Maschenka's beautiful hair, her remarks con-
sist in commanding her companion, a very
homely little Frenchwoman, by turns to
open or close a window.

After dinner the married couple quarrel over several immaterial trifles, which
momentarily interest no one; over the lat-
est Russian table of duties, and as to
whether it is better to treat scarlet fever
with heat or with cold. Then Varvara Pavlovna busies herself in her favorite occupation; that is to say, twisting paper flowers.
Natalie took part in this, but Maschenka, to
whom they have confided an album with
views of Dresden for her entertainment,
has uneasily crept about the room, now
reached after this and now that, has hopped
around first on the right, then on the left
leg, until at last Natalie's maid presents

herself to ask her mistress if she has anything to command or to be done, whereupon
Natalie has commissioned her to take the
little one out for a walk, and then to take
her to the Hôtel du Saxe.

Then Sergei read something aloud from
the newspaper ; then tea was brought.

It is nine o'clock. Natalie rises, says
that she is tired, and that she would like to
retire early to-night. Sergei asks: " Do
you wish to drive? Shall I send for a carriage? It would really be a shame ! The
evening is lovely; if you go on foot, I will
accompany you."

They go on foot. " I do not know what
fancy has seized me to loiter about a little,"
she says in the passage, where Sergei has
remained standing to light a cigarette.
" Would you have time?" she asks her
brother.

" Yes," replies he, " I am very willing to
walk a little. Where do you wish to go ?"

" Anywhere, where it is quiet and pretty,
and where one does not hear this café

chantant music." She points over the
Elbe, where from out a dazzlingly lighted
enclosure, frivolous dance measures sound
boldly and obtrusively over the dreamy
plash of the waves.

"Come in the fortress grounds," says
Sergei, and gives her his arm. And suddenly a kind of anxiety at being alone with
him overcomes Natalie. "Now he will
question me," thinks she, and would like to
tear her arm away from him and—has not
the courage to do it.

They are quite alone in the court-yard,
the world-renowned court-yard of the fortress, with its enclosure of strange, carved,
exaggerated, and charming irregular architecture; only the sentinel continually goes
along the same path, up and down, and
above, on the flat terrace roofs of the fortress, a couple of friends are walking. One
hears them laugh, jest; yes, even kiss,
standing in the court below. They may be
lovers, or some couple on their wedding tour.

The lanterns burn red and sleepily in the

transparent pale gray of the summer half light, and the buttons of the sentinel shine dully; all other light is extinguished in the world, but up in heaven the stars slowly open their golden eyes. What is there down here to-day for them to look at?

A thunder-storm threatens, but one does not see it as yet, but only hears its hollow voice growling in the distance.

Slowly the brother and sister wander along the narrow way between the old-fashioned, regularly laid-out flower-beds. The stony faces of satyrs and fauns grin down upon them with triumphant cynicism. One can still see their small eyes, slanting upward toward the temples, distinctly in the dull, shadowless, clear twilight. The air is sultry and close, and quite immoderately impregnated with the sad, penetrating perfume of weary flowers which have been tormented by an over-hot summer day.

"Do you remember the last time that we walked around here together?" remarked Sergei, at length breaking the silence.

"Yes," says Natalie. "It was the year before our father's death. I was not much older than Maschenka, and you had not completed your studies."

"Quite right, I did not yet feel myself obliged to be ambitious, in order to help raise our family from its sunken condition," said Sergei véry bitterly. "Father had taken me with him during my vacation, in order to cultivate my æsthetic taste. Only think, Natalie, at that time I wrote a poem on the Sistine Madonna! I! that is very laughable, is it not?"

"You—a poem," says Natalie, astonished, and still absently; the affair has in reality little interest for her.

"Yes, I—a poem!" repeats Sergei. "I —now at that time I was an idealist, however improbable that may seem to you! Now, now I am a machine, who still sometimes dreams of having been a man!" He laughs harshly and forcedly, and is suddenly silent. After a while he begins again: "Just look at the roses, Natascha," and he points to the slender bushes which are almost broken under their weight of dried blossoms. "Have you ever seen such an Ash Wednesday? Early this morning they were still fresh! It is a pitiless summer."

Natalie lowers her head. "Now it is coming," she thinks. "Now it is coming." But no, not what she has expected, but something different, comes.

"Did it ever occur to you," continues Sergei after a little while, "how very much a tree struck by lightning resembles one killed by frost? In the end it all tends in the same direction." He is silent. After a while he says, looking her straight in the eyes: "Did you understand me?"

"Yes, I understand," murmurs she, tonelessly.

"Hm! it was plain enough. You are dying of heat, I of cold!" says he, and laughing slightly to himself, he adds: "Do you still remember how I lectured you at that time in Rome?"

Instead of any answer, she pulls her hand away from his arm. Compassionately her brother looks at her through the gray veil of the now fast-descending twilight. "Poor Natascha!" he says. "You surely do not believe that I will return to my wisdom of that time—no! I will make you a great confession!" His voice sounds hissingly close to her ear. She feels his breath unpleasantly hot on her cheeks. "There are moments when I envy you!" he whispers. "Bah! that one must say of one's self: it is over, one is old, one will die, without once having been deeply shaken by a true shudder of delight,—*sans avoir connu le grand frisson*—it is horrible! I know what you have to bear, Natalie, and still—yes, there are moments when I envy you!"

"Who has then permitted himself to assert that I have anything to bear?" Natalie bursts out.

"Who?" Sergei raises his eyebrows. "You surely do not fancy that it is a secret?" says he. "Many wonder that you endure it ; as it seems, he exercises an incredible charm over all women !"

Her eyes and his meet in the sultry half darkness. "What have they told you?" asks Natalie, with difficulty.

But then he replies with fearful emphasis : " You surely do not demand an answer of me in earnest ? "

She breathes heavily. " It is not true !" says she. " They have lied to you !"

Thereupon he remains silent. The sultriness becomes ever more oppressive. Heavy thunder-clouds creep slowly and threateningly over the roof of the fortress and blot out the stars from the heavens.

Natalie has turned away from her brother, and with uneasy haste she hurries to the gate of the yard ; he comes after her. " I am sorry to have wounded you," he says. " I had not that intention."

She answers nothing ; silently she walks along near him. From time to time he pulls her gently by the sleeve and says : " This is the way." The stars are all extinguished, clouds cover the whole heaven, and close to the ground sighs a heavy wind which cannot yet rise to a hurricane. What is it in this depressing sound of nature which chases the blood more rapidly through her veins?

At the door of the great, many-storied hotel, Natalie wishes to take leave of her brother. " I will accompany you to your room," says Sergei.

Silently, she lets him remain near her. With bowed head she goes up the broad staircase to the first landing; then something wakes her from her brooding thoughts —the rustling of a woman's dress. She looks up—there goes a man up the stairs to the second story with a heavily veiled woman on his arm. She sees him for one moment only; then the shadow of his profile passes quickly over the wall; she turns away her head. It is he—she has recognized him! Silently and with doubled haste she follows her brother's guidance. " Your room is No. 53," says he, and turns the door-knob of a room. The lamp is lighted, everything cosily prepared for her reception. " I will disturb you no longer," says Sergei. His manner has become very stiff, his voice is icy cold, and before he leaves the room his glance seeks a last time the eyes of his sister.

.   .   .   .   .   .

She is alone. Trembling in all her limbs, she has thrown herself down on a sofa. The maid presents herself with the question whether her mistress wishes to undress. Natalie signifies to her to go away, to retire for the night to her room in an upper story. The maid goes, happy to be released from her service, weary, sleepy. Natalie does not think of sleeping. How should she think of it when she knows that here, under the same roof, a few rooms distant from her— It is horrible! It seems to her that she is slowly suffocating in a close, oppressing dread.

The lamp burns brightly. As a maid of good form, Lisa has already unpacked those little objects which luxurious women always carry about with them, even on the shortest journey, in order to make a hotel residence cosey. On the table lies Natalie's portfolio; her travelling writing utensils stand near by; and near the ink-case two photographs in pretty little leather frames—the pictures of her husband and of her son. Shuddering, she turns away. She pushes the hair back from her temples. "Sergei recognized him also!" murmurs she to herself. "It was impossible not to recognize him," whispers she, "and Sergei believes that I will still bear this also. And why should he not believe it?"

For years she has waded through the mire after a *fata morgana*, and the world laughs, and points its fingers at her. What does she care about the world, if she can only once shake off the feeling of boundless degradation which drags her down to the ground? In a few days he will come to her with loving glance, uneasily concerned about her, with a thousand anxious, tender words, with open arms. And she—well, she—she will rush into those arms, forgive and forget everything as before. Ah!—she springs up.

A few moments later she stands near the bed of her little daughter. The child looks very lovely in her white night-gown, richly trimmed with lace and embroidery. One of her hands rests under her cheek, the other is hidden under the pillow. Formerly Natalie has come every night to the bed of the child in order to kiss and bless her, still asleep. But to-night her tortured heart is capable of no tender emotion.

"Wake up!" she commands, in a harsh, strange voice. Maschenka starts up, thereby involuntarily drawing her hand out from under the pillow, and with the hand a little letter which she immediately tries to conceal again from her mother. But Natalie tears it away from her. "What have you to conceal from me?" she says to the little girl, imperiously.

"I have only written to papa!" replies

Maschenka excusingly, tearfully. " I wrote him that you are sad, and that he must come very soon because we will be so glad —that was all."

Natalie tears the poor little letter apart in the middle. " Dress yourself!" she orders.

" Is there a fire?" asks Maschenka, frightened.

" No, but something has happened; we cannot stay in the hotel; do not ask."

Sleepy, but obedient, as a good child who has the most complete confidence in her mother, Maschenka sets about putting on the clothes daintily arranged on a chair near her little bed. Natalie helps her as well as her fingers, trembling with fever, will permit her, then wrapping head and shoulders in a lace scarf, she takes the child by the hand and hurries down the stairs.

" Is the princess going out?" asks the porter, who has not the heart to give the sister of Prince Assanow another title.

"The weather is very threatening; shall I send for a carriage?"

Natalie takes no notice of him, pushes by him like a strange, inexplicable apparition.

.   .   .   .   .   .

The stars are all extinguished, clouds cover the whole heaven, and close to the ground sighs a weary wind.

What is it in this confused, depressing sound of nature which chases the blood through her veins? In the midst of her excitement she hears the chromatic succession of tones—her breath stops—it is that inciting, musical poison, that now follows her with a longing complaint, a strange, alluring call—Asbeïn.

The wind rises, screams louder and more shrill, its sultry breath rages so powerfully against Natalie that she can scarcely proceed. One, two great water-drops splash in her face, then more. Pointed hailstones prick her between them; all drive her back —back.

Has not some one seized her by the

dress? She looks round. No! she is alone on the street with her child and the raging storm. Forward she hastens, panting, breathless. The way to Bellevue is quite easy to find—quite straight along the street. It grows darker and darker, the rain falls in streams, the clothes hang ever heavier on her body, she can scarcely lift her feet from the paving; it is as if all would drag her down to the ground—all! Twice she loses her way, twice she suddenly, as if attracted by an evil charm, stands before the Hôtel du Saxe.

Maschenka cries silently and bitterly to herself. There—this wall ornamented with black lead, Natalie remembers, and here— the large mass of formless shadow—is not that the Catholic church?

A flash of lightning rends the darkness— Natalie sees the immense stairs of the Brühl terrace, with its adornments of colossal gilded statues; she sees the broad, black river flowing along, cool, alluring; hastily she goes across the place, for one moment her eyes rest on the stream—Maschenka pulls her by the arm with her tender little fingers, and whispers: "I am afraid, mamma; I am afraid!"

Then Natalie turns away from the most alluring temptation that has ever met her in life, and the water ripples behind her as if in anger that they have torn away a sacrifice from it.

Now they have reached the Hôtel Bellevue; the phlegmatic Hollander in the porter's lodge looks after her in astonishment as she rushes past him, stretches his powerful limbs, sticks his thumbs in the arm-holes of his vest, closes his eyes, sleepily, and murmurs, "These Russian women!"

She finds the number of her brother's sitting-room. Light still shines through the keyhole. She bursts open the door. Varvara Pavlovna is still busy making flowers. Sergei sits bent over a railroad courier, the eternal samovar stands on its small table.

"What has happened, Natalie, for God's

sake ?" says Varvara, as she discovers Natalie's figure, dripping with water, her pale, staring face, her burning eyes, and the little girl by her side. "What has happened?" The brother does not ask.

"I come to seek shelter with you," murmurs Natalie, breaking down, as she sinks upon a sofa; then turning to Sergei, she with difficulty gasps out: "You understand—I could not stay there—it—it is all over!"

.   .   .   .   .   .

Yes, it was all over—all. The bond between him and her was broken. He was beside himself when he discovered what had taken place, begged for a meeting, wrote her the tenderest letters. She left his letters unanswered.

Then a wild defiance overcame him. It angered him that she had placed herself under her brother's protection — that brother, who from the beginning had wished to sow discord between him and her. He also could not be persuaded that the prince had not alone been the cause of the separation.

The circumstance that Natalie travelled in advance with her sister-in-law to Baden-Baden, while Assanow remained in Dresden to arrange with Lensky, strengthened him in his conviction.

It did not come to a legal separation. Lensky was not the man to use compulsion with a woman; if she did not wish to stay with him, he let her go voluntarily. That she wished to keep the child with her was understood of itself; he could see the child from time to time, for a couple of weeks, on neutral ground. Nikolas, as one could not interrupt him in his studies, quite naturally remained with his father in St. Petersburg.

" All that is understood of itself; why lose words over it?" thought Lensky to himself, while he quite passively consented to all the propositions of the diplomat.

For what reason did the unendurable man remain sitting there and tormenting him?

Quite everything was wound up between them—it was afternoon, and the brothers-in-law sat opposite each other at a long table strewn with papers, in a large, gloomy room, with dark green damask hangings, in the Hôtel du Saxe. A pause had occurred.

"What does he still wish?" thought Lensky, and drummed unrestrainedly on the top of the table, while at the same time he gave a significant glance toward the door.

Assanow coughed a couple of times; at last he began: "In conclusion, I must touch upon a delicate point—the question of money. My sister formally rejects all assistance on your part, Boris Nikolaivitch, and wishes strictly to limit herself to live on her own income!"

Then Lensky flew into a rage: "And you have declared yourself agreed to that?" he cried, to his brother-in-law.

"I should have considered it undignified in my sister if she had wished to act otherwise!" replied Assanow.

Lensky clutched his temples with a gesture which was peculiar to him. "Ah! leave me in peace with your pasteboard dignity," said he, impatiently. "I cannot endure the word—a parade expression which means nothing—live on her own income— my poor luxurious Natalie—but that is madness, simply not possible! You are indeed her brother, but still you do not know her. Such a tender, guarded hot-house plant as she is! Why, she would die if she did not have what she needed."

"With the best will, I would not be able to persuade her to take anything from you," replied Sergei, earnestly.

"Not?" Lensky struck his clenched fist on the table. "Listen, Sergei Alexandro-vitch, you are not only pitiless, you are also stupid. If she will not take anything from me, deceive her a little, tell her that the rents of her estate have increased, that you have sold building land for her, or what do I know! With women that is so easy, es-pecially with her, poor soul!—who has

never understood the difference in appearance between ten rubles and a thousand—
but force the money upon her, she must
have it! And hear me! if you do not so
care for it that she takes it, then I will make
a scandal for you, and insist upon a legal
exposition!"

For a moment Assanow was silent, then
he said: "Good, I will arrange it!" with
that he rose and offered Lensky his
hand.

But Lensky refused it. "Let that go!
Between you and me there is no friendship.
After the 'service' which you have ren-
dered me such grimaces are repulsive."

"You are mistaken if you believe I would
have persuaded Natalie to the separation,"
assured the Prince. "Naturally, however,
as a conscientious man, I could not dissuade
her therefrom."

"Conscientious! Certainly, hangmen are
always conscientious—that one knows,"
murmured Lensky, and stamped his foot
on the ground. "Well, you will see what

you have done! Meanwhile—go. I will not longer bear it—go!"

.   .   .   .   .   .

When Assanow hereupon wrote Natalie in Baden that the affair was arranged with Lensky, and the separation declared he added, at the same time: "I feel myself obliged to say to you, that Lensky in this whole affair has acted not only honorably, but really nobly."

To his wife wrote Sergei at the same time: "I do not understand the man!—*figurez-vous* that I myself for a moment was *sous le charme.* What a depth of nobility is in this prodigy! His is an enormous nature!"

.   .   .   .   .   .

As long as the separation was still impending, as long as the conferences still lasted, a kind of restless life fevered in Natalie; she forced her being, naturally inclined to tender reliance and dependence, to an independent strength of will, of which no one had thought her capable.

But when the last word was spoken, the separation at length validly arranged, she fell into a condition of brooding sadness from which nothing more could rouse her.

For still three years she lived after the separation; three years, in which every hour endlessly dragged itself along, and which flowed together in the recollection into a single endless, cold, dull day; a day in that northern zone where the sun, with far-extending, weak, weary beams, tardily remains the whole twenty-four hours long, standing on the horizon, and grudges the night its refreshing darkness and the day its light.

Her torment reached an exquisite culmination when Maschenka, who idolized her father, and who, in her childish innocence, had no idea of the state of affairs, in the beginning incessantly and anxiously asked her mother little questions referring to the separation. Natalie gave her no answer, frowned and turned away her head. And sometimes Maschenka then became ungovernable and angry. Her little warm, loving heart could not understand why they had taken away her idol.

Once, Lensky asked for his daughter for two weeks. Maschenka, with her English governess, was sent to Nice to her grandmother, where Lensky daily visited her. When, loaded with presents, her heart full of sweet, tender recollections, she came back again to Cannes, where Natalie had meanwhile awaited her, with fearful obstinacy she insisted in relating to Natalie endless things about the goodness and lovability of the father, and especially how impressively and anxiously he had inquired after mamma. Her full, deep little voice trembled resentfully thereby, and an angry reproach darkened her large, clear child's eyes.

For a while Natalie was quite calm, then, without having replied a word to the child, she stood up and left the room.

Maschenka observed with astonishment how she tottered and hit against the furniture like a blind person. Thereupon the

child remained as if rooted to the ground,
with thoughtfully wrinkled brow, her little
hands glued to her sides, standing, staring
down at the carpet as if she there sought
the solution to the great, sad riddle which
so occupied her. Then with a short motion as if shaking off something, which she
had caught from her father, like so much
else, she threw her little head back and hurried after her mother.

Natalie had retired to her bedroom.
Maschenka found her deathly pale, with
helpless, stiff bearing, and hands folded
straight before her, sitting in an easy chair;
her weary glance, directed in front of her,
expressed inconsolable despair.

"Little mother, forgive me, oh, forgive
me!" begged the child, embracing her
mother with her soft, warm arms. "Sometimes it seems to me as if you love him as
much as I, only you do not wish to. But
why do you cover your soul with a veil;
why? Oh, why did you separate yourself
from him? He was not very much with

us without that, but still it was so lovely to expect him and to rejoice over him from one time to another!" And Maschenka burst out in violent weeping.

Natalie remained silent, but she raised the child on her knee and kissed her, ah, how tenderly! Every tear she kissed away from the round little cheeks. And Maschenka never repeated her question.

Once, in the night—Maschenka's little room was next to her mother's bedroom—the child awoke; from the adjoining room sounded soft, whimpering, difficultly restrained sobs.

.   .   .   .

She wandered from Venice to Florence, from Florence to Nice, from Nice to Pau—all the European cities of refuge for uprooted existences she sought out. Nowhere could Natalie find rest. Sometimes she tried to distract herself. She never visited large entertainments, but she associated with her old friends if she met them in their different exiles, gradually slid back into the old, aristocratic atmosphere in which she had been brought up; but, strange! she no longer felt at home therein, and in her inconsolable misery a feeling of insensible *ennui* mingled itself.

His name never crossed her lips. Did she ever think of him? Day and night. The more she tried to accustom herself to other people the more she thought of him. How empty, how shallow, how insignificant were all the others in comparison to him; how cold, how hard!

Her health went rapidly downward. A short, nervous cough tormented her, her hands were now ice-cold, now hot with fever. Associated with that was something else strangely tormenting: she almost incessantly had the feeling that her heart was torn away from its natural place; she felt in her breast something like an uneasy fluttering, like the beating of the wings of a deathly weary, sinking bird.

She slept badly and was afraid of sleep, for always the whole spring of her love, with its entrancing charm and perfume of flowers, arose in her dreams again. Again vibrated through her soul the swelling musical, alluring call—Asbeïn. Little trifles, which in her waking condition she no longer remembered, came to her mind, and when she awoke she burned with fever and hid her face, gasping, in her pillows. She consumed herself in longing; a longing of which she was ashamed as of a sin, and which she fought as a sin.

.   .   .   .   .   .

Gradually she became wearier and more calm. His picture began to obliterate itself from her memory.

.   .   .   .   .   .

It was in Geneva, in a music shop. Natalie, who had gone out to attend to a few trifles, entered and desired the Chopin Études, which she had promised to bring the extremely musical Maschenka. While a clerk looked for the music, she observed an elderly man—she divined the piano teacher in him—talking about a photograph which he held in his hand, to the woman who managed the business.

She glanced fleetingly at the photograph—she shuddered.

"So that is he; that is the way he looks now! *C'est qu'il a terriblement changé*," said the piano teacher.

"*Que voulez-vous*, with the existence which he leads?" replied the woman. "If one burns the candle of life at both ends!"

"But he should stop it, a married man, as he is," said the music teacher.

"My goodness; his marriage is so—so—he has been separated, who knows how long, already." The woman shrugged her shoulders.

"Ah! Who, then, is his wife?"

"Some great lady who has made enough out of him, and to whom he has become inconvenient," replied the old woman.

"So—h'm! that explains much," said the musician, and laying down the photograph, he added: "*enfin c'est un homme fini.*" With that he seized the roll of music which had been prepared for him and left the shop. Natalie bought the photograph, without having the courage to look at it before strangers. Arrived at home, she unwrapped the portrait. For the first time since that evening when she ran out of the Hôtel du Saxe she looked at a picture of him. She was frightened at the fearful physical deterioration designated in his features. Around the mouth and under the eyes hateful lines were drawn ; but from the eyes still spoke the deep, seeking glance as formerly, and on the lips lay an expression of inconsolable goodness. "A great lady who has made enough out of him, and to whom he has become inconvenient," Natalie repeated to herself again and again. That truly was false from beginning to end. Still, a great uneasiness overcame her. The reproofs which she believed she had expiated once for all by the easy, tender confession that she had set aside her beloved husband on account of her scruples, now rose sharply and reprovingly before her.

A nervous condition, which culminated in a long-enduring cramp of the heart, befell her; the cramp was followed by an hour-long swoon which could not be lifted.

· When she could again leave her bed, a great change had taken place in her. She no longer evaded the recollection of Lensky; the old love was dead, but a new love had risen from the ruins of the old, a new enlightened love, which was nothing more than a warm, compassionate pardon.

.	.	.	.	.	.

With the restlessness of those mortally ill, who in vain seek relief, she was again driven to leave Geneva, where at first she had intended to pass the whole winter. She longed for Rome.

The physicians laid no difficulties in the way. In the end, a dying person has the right to seek out the place where she will lay down her weary head for the last time.

.	.	.	.	.	.

In Rome, it seemed at first as if she would be better again. At the end of

March, Nikolas came to visit her. He was now a young man, tall, slender, with great dreamy eyes in an aristocratically cut face, and with pretty, still somewhat embarrassed manners.

Already he had twice come to foreign countries to visit his mother, but never had she been so glad to see him.

As the day was beautiful, and she felt better than usual, she proposed a drive. "To the Via Giulia," she ordered the coachman. "I will show you the Palazzo Morsini, in which we lived when your father was betrothed to me," she said to her children. Mascha looked at her mother in astonishment; it was the first time in quite three years that she had mentioned her father before her.

So they drove in the Via Giulia, on a bright March afternoon they drove there. But Natalie in vain sought the Palazzo Morsini; she did not find it. A pile of rubbish stood in its place, surrounded by a board fence. Disappointed almost to tears,

with that childish, foolish disappointment
such as only those mortally ill know, she
turned away. On the way, it occurred to
her to order the coachman to stop at the
Trevi fountain. She quite started with
delight when she saw the irregular collection of statues again. "Here I met your
father for the first time in Rome; it is just
twenty years ago," said she, and rested
a strange, brilliant, dreamy glance on the
old wall. The sculpturing was still blacker
and more weather-worn than twenty years
before, but the silver cascade rushed down
more arrogantly than ever in the gray stone
basin, and the sky, which arched over the
time-blackened walls, was as blue as formerly. "Ah, how much beauty, nobility,
and immortality there still is in the world,
together with the bad that passes away,"
murmured Natalie, softly; then passing her
hand over her eyes, and as if speaking to
herself, she added: "It is thus with great
men, and therefore I think, considerately
overlooking their earthly failings, one

should rejoice over that which is immortal in them!"

Maschenka had not quite understood the words, but Nikolas sought by a glance the eyes of his mother, and raised her hand to his lips.

It was evening of the same day, in Natalie's pretty apartment on the Piazza di Spagna, opposite the church of Trinità dei Monti, and the sick woman, relieved of her constricting and heavy street-clothes, lay, in a white, lace-trimmed wrapper, on a lounge. Mother and son were alone. He had read her a couple of verses from Musset, which she particularly loved—*les souvenirs*—but it had become dark during the reading; he laid the book away. For a while they were both quiet, silently happy in each other's presence, as very nearly related people when they are together after a long separation; but then Nikolas laid his hand on that of his mother and said, softly: "Little mother —do you know that it was really papa who sent me to you?"

The hand of the mother trembles, and softly draws itself out from under the son's. Nikolas is silent. But what was that? After a while his mother's hand voluntarily stole back into his, and the young man continued: "Yes, papa sent me here, so that I might accurately report to him how you are. You really cannot imagine how he always asks after you, worries about you."

The hand of the poor woman trembles in that of her son, like an aspen leaf. After a pause, quite as if he had waited so that his words might sink warmly and deeply into her heart, he continues: "Father commissioned me to bring before you a request from him—namely, whether you would not permit him to visit you?"

Again Natalie drew her hand away from her son, but more hastily than the first time. Her breath comes quickly and pantingly, for a few moments she remains silent, then she says slowly, wearily: "No! it must not be; tell him all love and kindness from me, and that I think only with emotion of the great consideration which he always shows me, but it must not be—it is better so!"

After she had made this decision, which had a sad and intimidating effect upon the inexperienced boy, she remained for the rest of the evening taciturn and with that, out of temper and irritable, as one had never formerly seen her.

In the night she had one of her fearful attacks; the doctor must be sent for. When the horrible oppression of breath and shuddering had subsided, as usual, she fell into a condition of pale, cold numbness, which resembled a deep swoon.

Nikolas, who had watched by the sick one, accompanied the physician without. He begged him, in the name of his father, to tell him the truth about the condition of the sufferer. The physician told him that her condition was very serious, and a recovery absolutely out of the question. It might last a few weeks still, perhaps only a few days.

When Nikolas, with difficulty restraining his tears, came up to his mother's bed, she lay exactly in the same position as when he left the room; still, something about her had changed. Her eyes were closed, but around her beautiful mouth trembled a smile whose happy loveliness he never forgot.

After a while she looked up and said in a quite weak voice: "Perhaps only a few days"—she had heard the doctor's speech. After a pause, she added: "Write your father—write—he must hurry—only a few more days!"

Nikolas telegraphed to St. Petersburg.

.　.　.　　.　　.　　.　　.

The consciousness of her near death had given her back her lack of embarrassment toward Lensky. She insisted that he should stay in her house, that they should prepare a room for him.

One day she was well enough to overlook the preparations herself. But the improvement did not last. Quite every night came on an attack, shorter and weaker, but still very painful; in between she slept, and always had the same dream. It seemed to her as if she could fly, but only about two feet from the ground; if she wished to rise higher, she awoke. Of the young happiness of her love, she dreamed never more.

   .   .   .   .   .   .

Lensky had telegraphed back that he would set out immediately. They counted the days and nights which must elapse before his arrival—Kolia and she; they consulted railroad time-tables together—so long to Eydtkuhnen—so long to Berlin—so long to Vienna—so long to Rome. They were twelve hours apart in their reckoning. Natalie expected Lensky already on the morning of the fifth day, Nikolas not until the evening.

On the fourth day she was so well that she wished to undertake a walk. " I would so like to see the spring once more," said she.

Nikolas begged her to save herself until his father had come, in order not to aggravate her heart by excitement—that great, rich heart through which she lived, and of which she was now dying. "We will bring the spring in to you," said he tenderly.

They brought flowers, whatever kind they could buy, and placed them in the pretty, pleasant boudoir in which she lay, stretched out on her couch bed. The broad sunbeams slid like a golden veil over the magnolias, violets, and roses.

Dreamily the dying woman let her eyes wander over the fragrant splendor. "How lovely the spring is!" murmured she, and then she added: "How can one fear to die, when the resurrection is so beautiful!" The windows stood wide open; it was afternoon; from without one heard the rattling of carriages which rolled along in the heart of the city.

It sounded like the rolling of a stream which forced its way to the sea.

.   .   .   .   .   .

The night came. Nikolas sat near his mother's bed and watched. She slept uncasily. Frequently she started and listened, then she looked at her watch—it could not yet be ! Once Maschenka came in, with little bare feet peeping out from under her long night-dress, and face quite swollen with weeping. On tip-toes she crept up to the dying woman's bed. Since a couple of days Natalie had no longer permitted her to sleep in the adjoining little room, from fear that the child might be awakened by her painful attacks. Maschenka had dreamed that her mother was worse ; she wished to see her mother. Natalie opened her eyes just as she entered.

Then the child ran up to her, kneeled down near her, and sobbing hid her little face in the covers. Natalie stroked her little head with weary, weak hand, and asked her to be brave, and lie down and sleep ; that would give her the greatest joy.

Then Maschenka stood up, and went with hesitating steps as far as the door ; then she turned round, and hurried back to her mother. Natalie made the sign of the cross on her forehead, then kissed her once more, and held her to her thin breast. It should be the last time—the child went.

Natalie looked after her tenderly, sadly.

Toward morning Nikolas fell asleep in the arm-chair in which he watched by his mother's bed. All at once he felt that some one pulled him by both sleeves. He started up; his mother sat half upright in the bed.

"Wake up, your father is coming!" she called quickly and breathlessly.

"But, little mother, it is quite impossible —not before evening can he be here."

With a short, imperious motion she admonished him to silence. Now he heard quite plainly—softly, then louder—the rolling of a single carriage through the deathly-quiet, sleeping city. It came nearer— stopped before the house.

"Go to meet him, Kolia; I do not wish him to think we did not expect him."

Kolia went, did, like a machine, whatever was required of him. Natalie sat up, list-

ened—listened. If she had been mistaken
—no. Heavy steps came up the stairs.
Steps of two men—not of one—and this
voice! rough, deep, going to the heart.
She did not understand a word; but it was
his voice.

A quite numbing embarrassment and
shyness overcame her. She drew the lace
cuffs of her night-dress over her thin arms,
she arranged her hair; she felt as shy as before a stranger. What should she say to
him? She would be quite calm—calm and
friendly. Then the door opened—he entered, dusty, with tumbled, badly arranged
gray hair, with fearful furrows in his face,
aged ten years since she last had seen him.

What should she say to him?

He did not wait for that; he only gave
one look at her pale face, then he hurried
up to her and took her in his arms.

Behind the church of Trinità dei Monti
there was already a golden light, and the
whole room was filled with brilliancy and
light.

"Oh, my angel! how could you so repulse me!" are the first words which he speaks.

She says nothing, only lies on his breast, silently, unresistingly. Through her veins creeps for the last time the feeling of pleasant, animating warmth which has always overcome her in his nearness. She tries to rouse herself, to consider; she had certainly wished to tell him something for farewell. But what was it—what——

Ah, truly!

"Boris," she breathes out softly, "do you know—at that time in your study—in Petersburg—do you still remember how you once said to me I should show you the way to the stars?"

"Yes, my little dove, yes."

"I was not fitted for my task," whispers she, sadly; "forgive!"

For one moment he remains speechless with emotion; then he presses his lips to her mouth, on her poor emaciated hands, on her hair.

"Forgive—I you! O my heart!" murmurs he. " How could you draw me up when I had broken your wings! But now all is well; we will seek our old happiness hand in hand. You shall become well, shall live!"

"Live," whispers she, quite reproachfully; "live," and shakes her head.

He looks at her with a long, tender glance, and is frightened.

Her face is still angel beautiful, but there is nothing left of her lovely form. It pains him to see the sharp, harsh lines which outline her limbs under the covering. That is no longer a living woman who stretches out her arms to him, it is only an angel who wishes to bless him. It is quite clear between them, and also the last shyness, which still held her back from him, has vanished.

"Yes, it is over," whispers she; "only a few more days—how many is that?—three days—five days—oh, perhaps it will last longer—physicians are so often mistaken. We will drive out once more together to

see the spring—out there where the almond
trees bloom between the ruins—by St.
Steven, do you still know?—and until I feel
it coming—the last, the end—then you will
hold me by the hand, will you not? like a
child that fears the dark, you will lead me
quite tenderly up to the threshold of eter-
nity—is it not true? No one can be so
tender and loving as you. But do not be
sad—not now; to-day I feel well, quite
well. Ah!——"

What is that? She clutches at her heart
—there it is again, the strange fluttering
feeling in her heart. Her face changes, her
breath fails.

"The doctor, Kolia!" calls Boris beside
himself.

Kolia hurries away; at the door his
mother calls him back once more.

"Not without a farewell, my brave boy,"
she says, and kisses him. "God bless you!"

Then he rushes away down the stairs, to
fetch the doctor—there is haste.

No, there is no more haste—the attack is

short—only a couple of strange shudders—
then the invalid grows calm in Lensky's
arms.

"How wonderfully the trees bloom—"
murmurs the dying one. "It grows dark
—give me your hand—do not grieve—my
poor Genius——"

Suddenly her eyes take on a peculiarly
longing expression. A last time the Asbeïn
tones glide through her soul, but no longer
an inciting, alluring call—but as something
elevating, holy. She hears the tones quite
high and distinct, as if they vibrated down
to her from Heaven, resounding strangely
in a sublime, calm harmony that is no longer
the devil's succession of tones, that is the
music of the spheres.

"Boris," she murmurs, and raising her
hand, points upward, "listen . . ."

The hand sinks slowly, slowly—when, a
little later, the physician enters she is dead.
A wonderful smile lies on her countenance,
the smile of one set free.